T WELLS BROWN

Lawyer & Lace

A Women of Wine Country Story

First edition

ISBN: 9781733330718

Proofreading by Donna Walker
Proofreading by Janette Shutts

This book was professionally typeset on Reedsy.
Find out more at reedsy.com

In loving memory, this book is dedicated to a cherished reader, mother, and beautiful woman Joanne Marie Culp. Her daughter, Virginia, introduced my books to her, and thankfully Joanne was able to attend The Last Witch's release party and Witch Walk last year where I was thrilled and honored to meet her.

My Cinderella would have preferred the pumpkins, the quiet little attic room with garden flowers in jars, and candlelit nooks for writing.

No crowded halls, or fancy glass, or rooms too big to breathe.

Just her man with a sword, her hair let down, and her loyal little creatures at her feet.

ANNA MARIE ELEAZER

Contents

Acknowledgement

When I say it takes a small village to bring my books to the point of publishing I'm not exaggerating. Luckily for me, I have a sister team that makes sure my books are as good as they can be. A huge thank you to Donna and Janette for the friendship and mentorship these two amazing women have brought to my life's work.

As always, a giant thank you to my husband Don, and son Brandon, for supporting me while I pursue my dreams.

1

I Take You

"No more delays," Roman's dark eyes fixated on me. You'd think I'd get used to hearing his deep raspy growl... and yet, it still made my toes curl.

"Babe, we can't announce a date. It's too soon."

I cringed when his dark eyes grew hard. I didn't like the look he was giving me.

I smirked inward.

He thinks I've lost my mind. I hadn't of course. Lost my mind that is. Well, not completely. I was pushing him to his limit and I knew it. Not on purpose. Never that.

I loved him, of that I was certain. But what he was asking for was impossible.

Had our wedding been postponed numerous times?

Yes.

But... always for good reason. That is, if murder and kidnapping were a good enough reason. And really, it wasn't like I didn't *want* to marry him. We were already living together for heaven's sake, in a gorgeous home surrounded by row after row of delicious wine-producing grapevines. We had a giant crystal-clear pool that I watched longingly through my floor-to-ceiling windows while working my fingers to the bone, in my plush home office. My law practice was humming along beautifully. To make it even more exciting, I'd have my first crop of grapes next year for harvest. I was so excited to learn how to make my own wine from the grapes I grew on my own land. After so many years of celebrating incredible wine produced by my friends, who were vineyard owners, it was finally my time.

But to add a wedding on top of it?

I took in his strong jaw and broad chest, and my expression softened.

Had he waited for me for six long agonizing years?

Yes, he had. It sucked that I had to lose so much time with my friends, family… and even him. But it couldn't be helped. I was living in Europe trying to stay alive after saving his life. It wasn't my fault that the people who tried to wipe his gorgeous butt from the face of the earth tried to wipe me out too.

Had he suffered through me being kidnapped by the worst of the worst not knowing if I'd survive?

Also, yes. But that wasn't my fault that I was abducted. It wasn't like I ran around looking for creepy bad guys to abduct me. These particular bad guys were too hideous to walk the earth. They did unspeakable things to innocent children and deserved everything they got. But *we* hadn't deserved any of it.

None of us had.

It's just that, too much had happened. The creepy bad guys *did* seem to keep finding us. No matter what measures we took to stay safe. After all, it wasn't like I had any control over *any* of it. The Russian Mafia, serial killers, wildfires, perverts, and crazy contractors; how was I supposed to compete with those types of evildoers? I couldn't make sense of it - much less expect my friends, my dearest sisters, to put their tragedies aside to celebrate my special day. Absolutely not.

"We have to postpone it!" My nerves were fraying. He couldn't possibly be serious. "Cabe and his men haven't even caught the guy who bugged all of our homes. It's not safe!"

Roman and I were having a standoff in our bedroom. I, medium build with a sweet bob cut I loved, and hazel eyes. My trademark red lips were perfectly lined and I was dressed in a soft sage pencil skirt and matching silk blouse. I hadn't slipped my beige pumps on yet so I was much shorter than I wanted to be if we were going to have a go.

"If we wait until every bad guy who has targeted you and your friends are caught, we'll never get married and that's not reasonable. I love you, Angel. I've been patient. I waited for you to come back and I've waited a year for you. I'm done waiting. I'm making the decision and choosing us before something else comes along."

We were facing each other across the bed with our hands on our hips; both of us charged for a fight. His giant form was dark and menacing. Wide shoulders, a broad chest (you know; the type that feels soft and hard all at the same time). He was ready to leave the house to start his day and I was about to head to my office which was located at the other end of our home; Avorio Manor. We'd moved in together the previous year, and he'd proposed. Well, technically he stated we were getting married while I was in the hospital, and then proposed after I got out of the hospital (after I sulked around a bit dropping hints that he needed to offer me a proper proposal). Like, you know, with a ring. But those were minor details.

"It's not our fault."

"No. It's not. But the threat of losing you is fresh in my mind. You're all I value in this world. I need you tied to me." He took a step closer and leaned forward. I mean… how do I get mad about the sexiest man I've ever known in my whole life wanting nothing more than to marry me? "No. More. Delays."

That's when I noticed his clenched teeth.

Now for Roman, this came out as a sexy growl which had me flushing and certain lady parts paying attention. Because let me tell you when it comes to that man and his deep gravelly voice I have less than zero control over my hormones.

Less. Than. Zero.

However, this was not his normal tactic when he wanted to win the favor of his future wife. Usually, he would romance me into giving in. He knew exactly how gullible I was when it came to his sexiness. Let's face it, on top of his voice, the man was drop-my-panties gorgeous.

And knew how to use it. Linebacker large with wide shoulders that seemed like they could carry the weight of the world, a broad chest, thick delicious thighs, dark hair, and pin-you-down green eyes surrounded by black lashes that were currently laser-focused on me.

I could tell by his stance and his set jaw, that this was going to be a real humdinger of a fight ... that is, if I let it get that far.

I stepped around the bed closer to him, and put my hands on his hips before I stepped further into him and laid my head right where it belonged... on his chest.

I moaned to myself when my cheek hit him. Hard and soft just like I said.

"It's not fair to the girls to not be ready for the big event. I can't ask them to halt their recovery after everything they've been through, to work on my wedding." I squeezed his hips hoping he'd go back to being reasonable-understanding Roman instead of this version of him I'd only seen glimpses of before.

I didn't think it was working. His hands were still on his hips and he wasn't cuddling me like he normally did when I was anywhere within arm's reach.

"Our wedding," he ground out.

I pulled back a smidge and looked up into his handsome face. "Hunh?"

"You said 'my wedding' it's our wedding."

"I'm sorry honey. I meant our wedding." I relaid my cheek against his chest.

"No, you meant your wedding. Tell ya what," he growled and moved me off of his chest before he leaned forward to place his face in front of mine.

I leaned back, keeping my hands on his hard chest. I'd never heard him start any sentence with "Tell ya what" and it didn't sound like one I was going to like hearing this time.

"You can have *your* wedding anytime - anywhere you like. As long as *my* wedding happens before Christmas." He planted a firm kiss on the middle of my forehead.

I couldn't have heard him correctly. Christmas was only a few weeks away.

My hands whipped from his hips to mine.

"I can't plan a wedding in a few weeks!"

I may or may not have stomped my foot. Couldn't be sure.

"You don't have to." My big beautiful man's hands pulled me back to him. This was more like it.

"I don't?" I rested my forehead on his broad chest and snuggled in wrapping my arms around his waist. This was definitely better.

"No, I'll take care of everything." He delivered another kiss, this time to the top of my head.

"How?" I asked snuggling further into my big man's body.

"I'll let Pete know to ready the jet and we'll go to Vegas this weekend."

"What?" I tried to pull away. He'd been sneaky however and wrapped his arms around me while talking, so I couldn't escape his clutches once I'd heard his evil plan.

The fiend.

"I'm not marrying you in Vegas. I want a fancy wedding with my friends." I pointed to the ground. "Here, where we're building our memories."

"Then you have until Christmas to organize it. If you haven't pulled it off by then you get my version of the perfect wedding which is no fuss, no friends, just us in Vegas."

Was he serious?

"You can't be serious!" I breathed. My mind whirling a million miles a minute. It couldn't be done. I'd have to find a way to convince him. This was madness!

"I'm absolutely serious. And Angel, I can hear your mind working all the angles. I'm telling you right now, if you try to pull a fast one on me, I'll hunt you down, plop that gorgeous ass of yours on our plane, and fly you to Vegas myself."

Lord Almighty! He was serious. And if I knew anything, I knew that when Roman Stognafsky said he would do something... something happened.

"Lemme go!" I shouted.

He held tighter. "I'm not fooling around, Sydney."

"I know!" I tried to pull away once more to no avail. "I need to get busy!"

He leaned back and looked me straight in the eye. I don't know what it is he was looking for or if he found it, but he offered me a small smile and planted a kiss softly on my mouth. I relaxed into his kiss until he pulled back and gruffed, "Christmas, Angel."

Reality crashed in on me, he wasn't going to budge.

"I heard you!" I panicked knowing I didn't have a second to waste. "I have so much to do. Do you have any idea how unreasonable this demand is?"

Instead of answering my question he kissed me one last time and left the room.

Damn.

I am not even a little embarrassed to say, as mad as I was; I watched that man's ass as he walked away. His backside was the finest I'd ever seen.

Looked like I was having a Christmas wedding.

2

To Have

After the crazy ultimatum… I mean *announcement* from Roman; it was clear that if I didn't get my rear in gear, I was going to have a Vegas wedding. That would *not work* for me …or my tribe, on so many levels.

I couldn't believe he was putting me under this kind of pressure. The man had no concept of what it took to make the perfect wedding come together. So many moving pieces and details that required weeks of thought, research, and finally, precise execution.

It was going to take every last one of us to pull this off.

I ran to my office in my bare feet. This was an emergency if I'd ever seen one and desperate times called for desperate measures. The first thing I needed to do was make a list. Mostly to organize my thoughts but also, I needed to know who was going to be available to take which part of my workload so I could focus on the event at hand.

My wedding. I mean, *Our Wedding…* shoot, I guess I was only thinking about what I wanted. The truth was Roman didn't seem to care about the wedding much. He just wanted to be married. The wedding was for me.

How could he be so thoughtless?

I ripped off the paper and started a new list. I wrote the heading in big scrawl across the top of the page; *Why Roman Sucks!!!*

Doing that made me feel a little better so I went back to the first list regarding the wedding.

This was supposed to be the ceremony I'd always dreamed of. One I honestly never thought I'd ever have. I mean, I was way past your typical bride's age. Here I was, a mature woman with a successful import-export law firm and many accomplishments under my belt. But anytime I thought about it - it was always the same; when it came right down to it, I wanted the same things any other woman wanted who was getting married.

Perfection.

I didn't think the perfect wedding was too much to ask for. Not too much at all. Therefore, I did what any successful woman my age would do after finishing the long detailed list for the perfect wedding... I started crying.

This was an impossible task. I stopped crying and moved right on to mad. How could he put this kind of pressure on me? It wasn't fair. I added a few more items to the *Why Roman Sucks!!!* list but only felt marginally better.

I stomped my foot and then turned my desk chair around to gaze out the glass wall overlooking our Olympic-sized pool. I sniffled, wiped my nose, and made a decision.

Probably the smartest one I could have made... I don't know why I'd put it off. It was time to call in the troops. My tribe. I started crying again because I knew they'd understand.

I found my phone through my tears and located the contact I needed first.

"Hey sister," Terra, one of my oldest and dearest friends, answered.

"Hey," I hiccuped, followed by a sniffle.

Hearing the tears in my voice placed Terra on high alert. I could feel her energy through the phone, I knew her so well. I felt a little better already.

"What's going on?" I heard the jingle of keys.

"Roman!" I started crying again.

"Where are you?" She sounded a little out of breath.

"Home!" I was sobbing now.

"On my way, babe." And she was gone. I never even had a chance to tell her why I was crying. All she knew was I was in tears and it had to do with Roman and that was enough.

Next up was Isabella. She had two babies to deal with so it would be much harder for her to rush over but she was going to be integral to the reception. I needed her.

I found her contact on my phone as several texts came through, one right after the other.

Becca; *Finishing up with a feral cat feeding and then I'm on my way. I've got Francesca.*

Next Stella; *Jules and I are heading over now, sister. Whatever it is, we've got you.*

Jenna; *In my car almost there. xoxo*

Then lastly a text from Sloane; *Isabella is rustling the kids up now and we'll be over. We both love you!*

Terra had activated the tribe.

I started crying again because it felt so good to know I had such dear friends who would drop everything to rush to my side. These were tears of joy.

Then I felt bad because with everything that had been going on with us - maybe the wedding drama wasn't the most important thing I could have activated the tribe for.

Who was I kidding? Of course, this was the most important thing I could activate the tribe for! It wouldn't take my girls long to arrive so I headed toward my front door.

With that last thought, true to her word, Terra's sporty little Mercedes roadster squealed to a stop in front of my house and I watched as my stunning Greek goddess of a friend flew out of her car and ran on her heels to my front door where I awaited her arrival.

She was thin, disgustingly thin, and appeared tall. She wasn't any taller than me but she wore shoes with no-less than six-inch heels exclusively. This gave her added height in an extremely stylish manner. Her look was edgy class and she rocked it. Shiny black hair that fell around her shoulders and was teased within an inch of its life. She had perfect porcelain skin with large dark cat eyes she'd enhanced with perfectly applied black eyeliner.

Once she reached me, she grabbed my arms, and looked me over, before hugging me tightly.

"This emergency emotional, not physical?" She asked.

I nodded my head and she let out a deep sigh, and hugged me tight while whispering, "Thank God."

Jenna's suburban pulled into my drive with a repeat of Terra, she flew out of her vehicle and ran the entire way to where we stood watching her. She was the prettiest woman I'd ever seen. And she should be. She worked hard at her appearance and spent a wad on it too. Jenna was on her way back from a terrifying experience, but because of it, she'd found the man of her dreams so she was walking on cloud nine. That is unless one of her friends was in trouble.

Jenna had long silver hair, a small lithe build, and big green eyes. From the top of her perfectly coiffed head all the way down to the tip of her bright pink toes, every inch of my sweet sister was beauty personified.

She reached the two of us and embraced the hug.

"I'm so happy you're okay!" Jenna mumbled to my shoulder.

"I'm not okay. I'm upset! You wouldn't believe what Roman is making me do."

My tears began to fall quicker which made me chatter nonsense at the ladies as the rest of my tribe arrived. I was trying so hard to tell them what was going on but as I started to calm down another of my friends would show up and each new arrival made me emotional. Finally, Isabella and Sloane got there and we shuffled into my kitchen.

"Alright. Since I can see that Sydney's body isn't injured, I need to know what the drama is about so I can decide if I'm getting invested or not," Becca said to the group.

"Becca!" Jenna admonished.

"What? Everyone I care about in the world is alive and well and sitting in this room with me. I need to know if this new development is something I can help with or not." She looked at me. "Spit it out, sister."

"Roman says I have to plan our wedding before Christmas or he is whisking me away to Vegas to get married and I won't have any say about it," I shouted and slapped my palms down on my island to hold myself up.

"What? Christmas is only...." Jenna held her hand up and counted on her fingers, "this many weeks away!"

Terra braced herself on the island mimicking my stance and breathed, "Four weeks? We have four weeks?"

"Wait. Wait just a minute." Jenna shook her head. "Did he say the wedding had to *be* before Christmas or the planning of it had to be done by Christmas?" That was my girl. Always looking for a loophole.

"He said we had to be married by Christmas. If not, I'm having a Vegas wedding!" I started crying again.

"He can't be serious. I have so many holiday parties and banquets. How am I supposed to be able to design, plan, shop, and bake not only a wedding cake fitting for Sydney and Roman but the food for the reception too!" Isabella might be almost as upset and freaked out as I was.

"He isn't being reasonable," Stella blurted out.

"I agree. Surely there is some way to convince him." Jules looked at me with big eyes.

"Trust me I tried everything!" I gave her big eyes back. I'd caught her gist.

"Why can't we just go to Vegas?" Every head turned to Becca. She looked around at us and seemed to realize she'd stepped in it but wasn't sure why.

"Seems like it would be fun to me." Becca shrugged her shoulders.

"This is outrageous!" Terra dug through her purse.

"Let's get something straight. He didn't say, "let's take all your friends and go get hitched in Vegas." He said, 'I'm gassing up the jet and the two of us are flying to Vegas'."

"No!" Jenna said. "He wouldn't dare!"

"He would!" I replied.

"This is getting us nowhere." Terra was on her phone typing away.

"Francesca, can we still have it at your place?" Terra wasn't wasting time.

"Of course," Francesca replied. "I've already got the arbor up. But all the plants are dying off and everything will be dormant soon."

"If Isabella could do the cake, we could find another caterer to handle the food," Terra said without looking up because she was typing furiously on her phone.

"I'm providing the cake and the food!" Isabella grabbed her phone and began typing feverishly until her phone rang and she stepped away to answer it.

"If you think you can handle it..." Terra still hadn't looked up to see Isabella wasn't standing there.

"I said I've got it!" Isabella covered her phone. "You think I'm allowing anyone else's food to be served at Sydney and Roman's wedding? You don't know me very well!" When she went back to her phone call, I let out a sigh of relief. I knew it was going to be hard for her but I also knew I didn't want anyone else's food but Isabella's at my wedding.

"Jenna, do you think you can rustle up a wedding gown and bridesmaids' dresses in less than four weeks?" Terra asked.

"Wait. Who's the matron of honor?" Jenna had eyes on me while nodding to Terra.

"I," I looked around at the faces of my very best friends and knew at that moment I had no idea. Or any idea how I was going to choose one of these incredible women over another.

"I always thought if I ever got married that Raquel would be my maid of honor and Antonio would walk me down the aisle." I looked around again, "I mean I'm not twenty. How is it going to look if I have a huge wedding party?"

"Honey, can I make a suggestion?" Stella placed her hand over mine.

"Of course," I said.

"Ask Sophie to be your maid of honor."

I could tell from the reaction around the room that the other ladies thought this was a good idea, too.

I thought it was perfect.

I took Stella's hand in both of mine and kissed it. "I think that's a fabulous idea."

"We're all going to be way too busy to be members of the wedding party anyway." The way Terra was working her phone I was sure it was going to catch on fire.

"Jenna, we are still going to want dresses that match the wedding. Can you handle that on top of Sydney's dress?" Terra finally looked up from her phone to make eye contact with Jenna.

"I can probably do it. I'll need to know what styles and colors we are looking at." Jenna owned a fashion company and outfitted all our themed parties and fundraisers. She was top-notch.

"Becca, Stella, and Jules you're in charge of decorations," Terra said and looked to Sloane, "You're in charge of the bar and music."

The ladies nodded in agreement for their assigned duties.

"Okay, now we need the date and theme and we can get cracking. What's it going to be Sydney?"

I knew exactly what I'd always dreamed of.

3

To Hold

"I want a white Christmas wedding!" I shouted to my friends who were standing around my kitchen island.

"Babe, you know that ship sailed years ago...right?" Becca snickered with big eyes.

Smartass.

"I mean, I want a Christmas wedding and I want it to be a white Christmas." I'd postponed my wedding three times, I was being forced into a deadline, and dammit, I deserved to have whatever kind of wedding I wanted!

"Not to keep bursting your bubble babe, but you know you live in central California where it doesn't snow... like... at all?" Becca was doing her part with her role in the tribe, and that was making sure we all kept our feet planted firmly on the ground. Even if the reality of her words hurt, they were where our lofty goals and lifelong dreams came to die.

She was a giver like that.

Ignoring Becca, I went to my wine bar and pulled out a bottle of my best bubbly. It was time to celebrate. I was getting married. For real. I grabbed a few glasses and went back to the island to pop the champs and pour a round.

"Cheers!" We clicked our glasses before taking a sip.

"I can give you a version of a white Christmas," Terra said quietly.

In unison, our heads swiveled to her.

"We can do a sea of white poinsettias and a forest of flocked Christmas Trees. We'll decorate the poinsettias with gold and silver glitter and the same with the trees. Crystals, strings of pearls, white lights; and if we do it outdoors, it'll be cold enough we could wear white faux fur." Terra took another sip of her champagne and looked at the open-mouthed friends who had gone silent when she'd started speaking, she wove a vision none of us thought possible.

"If we have it at Francesca's we can set up a champagne fountain, and an icy vodka bar to celebrate Roman's Russian heritage."

"Won't an ice bar and a flocked forest be expensive?" Jules asked.

"I have money," I breathed. I was in awe of the vision Terra weaved before me. A glistening holiday wonderland. I wanted it. All of it... and more. "Roman has more money than me. We can do whatever we want." I turned to Francesca. "As long as Francesca is okay with the wedding being at the Four F Ranch?"

I caught her as she was taking a sip from her crystal flute. She set the glass on the island and rose to embrace me. "Sister, you can do whatever you want at my ranch. The girls and I would be honored to have your wedding there."

Not wanting to be left out, Becca decided she could contribute too. "What about horse-drawn carriage rides?"

"That would be perfect. We can set up parking in the north field and bring the guests to the wedding via carriage." Terra was on a roll. The vision was forming and we were all getting excited.

Me especially. Since it was in fact, my wedding we were discussing.

"We can place bare branches in urns and set them around for greatest impact. We'll drape them in white lights, string them with pearls and crystals." Terra looked around the room again. Her eyes met mine and when she saw that tears were about to fall, she smiled. I let the tears stream and smiled back.

"Who will walk you down the aisle?" Stella broke the silent moment between Terra and me.

I looked around the room at my beautiful friends.

"I always thought if I ever got married, Antonio would escort me down the aisle," I replied.

We were silent as we sipped from our glasses.

"We can set up a special tree with all of the ornaments and tree skirt we had made from Raquel's wedding dress if you like?" Isabella interjected.

I reached over and squeezed Isabella's hand. I loved how seamlessly she fit in with our group. "That sounds wonderful."

"I think Sophie is perfect for my maid of honor. But I want you all to be as much a part of this wedding as Roman and I."

"Trust me, we will be," Sloane said and we all laughed.

I looked around at the women surrounding me. Sloane was new to the group and stayed quiet during most of these conversations. The rest of us had been friends for decades and knew each other's skills like we knew our own. I wasn't sure exactly what Sloane's skill set was other than being freakishly smart in a shy bookworm sort of way. Long strawberry curls cascaded from a high ponytail she wore most of the time. She was small, strong and freakishly smart.

"Are we going for a traditional Christmas theme of red and green?" Jules asked.

"I'm seeing champagne, rose gold, silver, and gold, accenting a sea of white and cream," I said. Terra gave me big eyes and a giant smile. I took that as a good sign. The other ladies sighed in a way that told me they too could see the romantic picture we were creating.

"The reception can be a long thirty-foot table, with the food placed on the center, family style. The wedding party and their plus one can sit at it," Terra said. "How many people do you think you'll have?"

I looked at her. "I think it'll be around Christmas so the guests who come will be much fewer than at any other time of the year. Don't you think?" I glanced at my friends for clarity. I wasn't really sure who would be willing to spend Christmas Eve sitting outside in the freezing cold at the 4 F Ranch, for my wedding. Maybe a lot of people, but also maybe not many. How could I know?

"We'd better start the guest list so we can get the invites out and find out how many people will be attending." Terra was on it. I guess I knew who my wedding planner was. I smiled to myself; like I even had a choice.

"I like the idea of incorporating the bare branches, and trees, with the pearls and crystals. They'll balance each other," Sloane said. "Let's bump them up even more and grow crystals on their tips."

I looked at her and smiled. She didn't speak up too much but was starting to more and more and I was going to encourage her. She had secrets behind her eyes that she hadn't shared with the tribe yet. Maybe Isabella had an inkling of what she was hiding but so far I didn't think the rest of the ladies knew much. I know I didn't. Nothing more than what her background check had produced when we'd hired her as Isabella's winemaker for Bellini Estate.

She'd earned Cabe and Isabella's respect as their winemaker, they'd reported she was the hardest-working person they'd ever met. That was saying something with this crew.

"Christmas Eve," I announced. "It's going to be Christmas Eve at dusk so the lights will shine and the crystals will sparkle. We'll need a ton of candles too. Everyone here okay with spending Christmas Eve with Roman and me?"

"I can't think of a better way to spend it," Sloane smiled and clinked her flute against mine.

"Don't you think we'll be cold?" Becca asked.

"I can make sure the gowns come with some type of jacket," Jenna said.

"We can place fire pits, torches, and heaters around too," Francesca offered.

"Would Faith be willing to be my flower girl?" I asked Francesca quietly.

"I think she'd be over the moon thrilled!"

"Well, I guess that does it. We have our time, date, and our theme. Now we need to get to work!" Terra was already back to work on her phone.

"Fine. If I'm missing a trip to Vegas and am expected to be at Francesca's for Christmas Eve, I'll expect gifts from you bitches!" Becca shouted.

"Don't call us bitches! Your gift from me is your damn dress!" Jenna exclaimed. "And you're gonna be happy about it!"

"Fine." Becca spent the rest of the day sulking while we planned. Little did she know we had already planned the biggest Christmas present her huge heart could ever want.

4

From This Day

Before the ladies left, Terra tasked me with two immediate items.

One, my guest list, and two, my dress. As soon as my girls left, I set to work on both straight away. I had a pad of paper next to my monitor and was browsing wedding dresses online. Jenna needed some images of what I liked so she could create a one-of-a-kind Jenna White wedding dress.

As I was browsing, whenever I thought of someone I wanted to invite, I'd add them to my list. I'd been sitting at my desk for a couple of hours and had a page and a half of names but wasn't anywhere close to finding the perfect dress when I saw Roman's car pull into the driveway.

It had been very difficult to control my impulse to call him right away. It would have burglarized his day, and he needed to keep his wits about him. I wasn't making any promises as the wedding planning grew more intense that I'd be able to control myself but I was going to try my best.

I continued on with my task. By the time Roman entered my office seeking me out I was bouncing in my chair.

I couldn't wait to tell him about our plans.

"Hey Angel, whatcha working on?" He asked entering my dark office.

"Stop!" I screamed and shoved to my feet. Roman was a smart man. Maybe a little too smart. He knew me like the back of his hand. He watched me for a quick minute and whatever he read on my face had him lean his shoulder against my door frame, cross his ankles, and shove his hands into his pockets.

Whew, that was a close call.

I needed him to stay there. I couldn't have him looking over my shoulder and seeing the types of dresses I was looking at. I wanted him to be overwhelmingly surprised when I walked down the aisle towards him in whatever I decided was the perfect dress for me to walk down the aisle to the man of my dreams in.

I put my hands up. "You can't see what's on this computer screen."

He wasn't in love with that statement and pushed off the door frame losing his relaxed stance. I was afraid he'd rush into the room and ruin everything so I moved around my desk and made my way to him. I knew I was pushing his buttons a little, but I was feeling a tiny bit like he deserved it. However, I didn't want to make him mad, so I slowed my stroll and tried to look as sexy as I could.

All this did was put him on edge and by the time I reached my guy, he was looking at me in a guarded, wary way. I didn't much like that either. I wanted him loose and happy. But I still wanted to punish him a little too. How to get what you want and still rake your man over the coals you might ask?

Watch and observe.

"What are you up to Sydney?" He growled in his sexy-as-sin deep voice. He looked down at me without reaching to pull me into his arms. Not a good sign. Roman rarely let me anywhere near him without drawing me into his personal space.

"I picked the wedding date and time." I reached him and put my left hand against his chest to admire my engagement ring as it caught the light.

"I picked the theme and I am currently," I pointed behind me toward my computer screen, "looking for wedding dresses I like."

He put his hands on my waist and pulled me to him.

See. Told ya he liked me in his space. I guess, when he wasn't afraid of what I was up to however. Good to know. I made a mental note to keep that in mind for future possible arguments. This info would also come in handy whenever I needed to get my way.

My big man wrapped his arms around me and rested his chin on the top of my head.

"Lay it on me."

And boy did I ever lay it on him. I laid it on him really good and thick. I talked without taking a breath for a solid twenty minutes. I told him everything. All about the white wedding, which girl was responsible for what, and that Terra was a dream maker.

"So, it's all hands on deck. No time to waste. I need your checkbook from this point forward," I finished, took a deep breath, and pulled back to gauge his reaction.

I wasn't done though. "Also," I dropped my voice to just above a whisper, "I'm asking Sophie to be my maid of honor. None of the girls are standing up with me." Something about this still didn't sit right. I didn't know if I should dive into it or let it go and worry about more important things.

But these were my sisters. What could be more important than them?

See. I couldn't get it out of my head.

"I don't see how that's going to work. Have you told them?"

"Yes…," I started.

"Well? What did they say?" Roman asked when I didn't continue.

"They said whatever I wanted."

"Was it your choice?"

"I just feel stupid at my age having a giant bridal party."

"Is there an age limit?" I could have sworn I detected a hint of laughter in his voice. I pulled back to look at him. Didn't see any indication he was laughing, but I squinted my eyes to let him know he was on notice.

"There's no age limit per se, but I don't want to be embarrassed… I guess. It's not like I'm in my twenties or even my thirties."

"Look, I don't always agree with everything you girls do but I do know they'd die for you and that's not just normal friendships. Seems like a small thing to have them in our wedding, and it's no one else's business. Anyone who doesn't get it doesn't know the friendships you have with each other and that sucks for them, and probably shouldn't be invited to our wedding anyway." Oh my God, this man was so smart. He was *literally* the voice of reason. Unless that is, I didn't agree with him then he was just wrong. But I totally agreed with him on this.

"This from the man who wasn't going to let my friends come to our Vegas wedding?"

"That wasn't just a Vegas wedding, that was my version of a perfect wedding. A quick ceremony and then five full days locked away in a suite with you, an in-room hot tub, a private pool, and room service. Your friends don't fit into the equation. But this is now, and it's your perfect wedding; that involves them, and it should."

"You just described a honeymoon. You want the honeymoon." I squinted at him. "Where are we going on our honeymoon?"

"Let's finish this discussion about the girls standing up with you."

"We don't call it that."

"Whatever you call it, they should be there in every way to support you."

"Of course. I don't know why I thought any different." My stomach dropped. "Roman, I said it out loud to them. I told them it would be embarrassing to have them in my bridal party!" What had I done? How could I have been so insensitive? Were they relieved or did I hurt their feelings? I needed to fix this!

Oh, Lord Almighty! This was going to be a long four weeks.

I laid my head on his hard chest and took a breath. This man's scent was something else. I moved my hands down to his well-defined ass and grabbed hold.

"I need you to quiet my head. Distract me for a while so I can think about what I truly want."

"Just a little while?" He was teasing me and that was good. Roman often teased me when he was feeling frisky. It was part of his love language. I released a satisfied sigh and looked up into his gorgeous green eyes.

"Christmas Eve is good for you then?" I whispered and trailed my hands over his chest.

"Sounds perfect," he whispered back.

"What did you think about the vodka bar?"

"I think it's perfect. What made you go with vodka?"

"Terra thought it would be a nice homage to your Russian heritage." I ran my hands around his chest to his back and squeezed.

"Then we'll need to have good Russian vodka to stock it."

I'd moved my hands back down to his perfect ass and became distracted. He was one of those guys who had a nice meaty ass and thick thighs and I could easily distract myself on this man and his body all day and night. I traced my hands along the lower back dip, up his wide back, and across his broad shoulders. They were my weakness. This is why I needed to make him mine.

"Why don't you get busy quieting my mind?" I mumbled.

He bent at the knees and placed his hands on my hips lifting me. I hiked my skirt to my waist before I wrapped my legs around his midsection. It felt good that he held me up easily. My head slightly higher than his, I placed my hands on his cheeks and held his face while I kissed him thoroughly, as he walked us to our master bedroom.

I lived for nights like this.

5

Forward

S ex with my man was one of the reasons I wanted to pin him down. Figuratively speaking that is. Roman was easily twice my size so pinning him down *literally* would take superhuman strength. And let's face it; I hardly had normal human strength.

For the record, pinning him down with his cooperation was one of my favorite pastimes.

Roman rarely did anything partway. He was an "all-in" kinda guy. When he devoted himself to anything or anyone, he became a full expert on that thing... or person.

Luckily for me, this man of mine had taken the time needed and was an expert at what I liked and didn't like, in all areas. He'd even discovered a few things I didn't know I'd like, but he did. And *Lord Almighty* did I ever like the things he'd introduced me to, once he'd convinced me to try them, that is. I also enjoyed the entire process of him getting to know my body.

Gives me butterflies to think about it.

He walked us to our room and kicked the door closed behind us. We never wanted to worry about our adopted daughter Sophie, walking in on us. There were just some things you didn't want to be seen.

Especially by your children, adopted or otherwise.

Besides, Sophie had been through way too much in her short life to be assaulted with the image of her parents having sex. She wasn't a child, she was a young adult... but still. Better safe than sorry, I always say.

Roman placed me on the bed and lowered his large body. I loved that first moment when his weight pressed against mine. The feeling of my big strong man on top of me... I couldn't explain it but I felt the thrill of danger and a rush of security simultaneously. It rarely lasted long because my large beautiful man was hyper-aware of my physical well-being. Being the security-conscious man of the law that he was, he worried about crushing me to death. Sometimes it seemed like half his mind during our intimate time was focused on not harming me.

Knowing him, it probably was. He was a hero like that.

I tried to hold him to me when he lifted away. My attempts were futile of course, like I said, he was almost twice my size. I watched him rise above me with his knees straddling my hips, he leaned back on his heels. Then he did my second favorite thing and ripped his shirt over his head in one quick movement, exposing his naked chest.

It took every bit of my restraint not to clap with glee. He was that gorgeous. Taking in his thick muscles and broad shoulders, I wondered if after twenty or so years of seeing him rip his shirt over his head - would it still have the same effect on me? Would I still see him the same way?

I shook my head. The truth was, I was positive I would. I couldn't think of anything that could possibly dim the love I had for my brave man, my soon to be husband... the love of my life. I never wanted to know another day or night without him.

I was finally home.

Finally.

Goosebumps ran over my heated body. I knew I was about to lose my mind to ecstasy, something I looked forward to, but also wanted to slow down, to savor the moment. This magnificent man was all mine, and he took pleasure anytime he gave me pleasure. I watched him through my lashes as he removed my yoga pants. Then he moved to my shirt.

I shivered.

He watched my reaction closely as he trailed his rough fingers across my breasts, paying extra attention to my nipples.

"Put your arms above your head and hold on to the headboard," he grumbled. I happily complied with his request. After all, he'd never steered me wrong.

"If you let go, I'll stop." His voice was husky. I shivered again, nodded my compliance, and wiggled my bottom a little. I couldn't control myself. I knew this was going to be good.

Roman lowered his head to my chest, and I watched his green eyes roam over my breasts. He took one of my nipples into his mouth and sucked. He flicked it with his tongue and then sucked again.

HARD.

Like, super hard. I immediately felt myself become wet, well, wetter, I was already so aroused it wasn't going to take much for me to shoot off like a rocket.

Back and forth he went, first one breast, then the other. My nipples quickly became highly sensitive and my breasts; full and heavy.

I loved it... and it took me to the edge of passion and then to where pain began. I waited as long as I could but I had to make him stop soon. As it was, my nipples would remain sensitive for a couple of days. I liked that too. The memory of our intimacy stayed with me when my nipples brushed up against fabric. Occasionally, I'd become so over-sensitized that I couldn't stand to wear a bra.

Those were the best times.

"Roman," I groaned, wiggled my hips but didn't let go of the headboard. I'd never let go until he said I could. He was, after all, a man of his word. If he said he'd stop, trust me, he would, I'd already put it to the test.

He spent a few more minutes on my nipples and then squeezed my breasts, before using his fingers to pluck at my over-sensitized nipples. My back arched off the bed and I moaned. I maintained my grip on the headboard like my life depended on it.

Roman worked his way down my body peppering light kisses along the way until he reached my feminine core. I was soaked. I could feel wetness on my thighs. And because of the extensive nipple play my vagina felt swollen and needy. If he slid into me at that moment, it would be a tight delicious fit. I watched waiting for him to rear back once more and remove his pants, but he didn't. I was laid bare before him. My hands firmly gripped the headboard, while Roman still wore his pants. I felt erotically vulnerable.

I shivered again.

I was anxious for him to take his pants down and enter me. He would typically slide in with one aggressive thrust so I'd learned to brace for it. It never hurt, but it always took my breath away.

But what came next was not his large hard cock driving into me. It was his warm wet mouth covering my vagina and sucking, hard. Just like he'd done to my nipples. I moaned and almost let go of the headboard but caught myself just in the nick of time.

Lord Almighty!

I moaned again as he placed his finger and thumb at my opening and spread my folds in a way that allowed him to have easier access to my clitoris.

He ran his tongue over the sensitive bud and went up, and down bringing me right to the edge of an orgasm and then changed pace or slowed down. He did it until I became so sensitive it started to hurt. I was so damned close to going off I raised my hips, and he stopped again. He blew on my wet swollen vagina and then sucked me into his mouth, flicking it with the tip of his tongue. I raised my hips again indicating I was going to orgasm, and he stopped and blew.

Dammit.

"Please," I moaned. That must have been what he wanted to hear because finally his mouth worked its magic, and I came on a shout that sounded something like, "Thank you, Lord!"

I know this because my gorgeous man countered with, "Thank you, Roman."

I wasn't sure what he was saying because my mind and body were still in the bliss zone. You know that time where the rush from your orgasm makes your entire body tingle, and all is right with the world? Yeah, that's where I was.

Anyway, I furrowed my brow and looked at him. "What?"

"You said thank you, Lord. But you meant thank you, Roman," he said as he crawled up the bed and my body. That's when I noticed he was still wearing his pants. I needed to do something about that.

"Yeah, whatever." My voice was kinda breathy.

I then made the fatal mistake of letting go of the headboard to unbuckle his belt in my haste to help him out of his trousers. To be honest, I never dreamed this would violate the "don't let go of the headboard" command but apparently, it did.

Looking back, my first indication that it was a problem was when his body went rigid. I wasn't paying close enough attention, however, or I would have been prepared for what came next.

Roman grabbed my hips, and in his deep gravelly voice, "You weren't supposed to let go, Angel."

I had just enough time to brace myself when he put his shoulder to my stomach and flipped me over said shoulder, lifting us both off the bed in one smooth move. Next thing I knew I was being carried fireman style out of my room, through my French doors that lead to our huge pool and then he...flung me.

Yes, that's right. Flung. Me.

Like, flung my naked ass into our pool. I was shocked and started to get a little pissed when I came up sputtering to the surface just in time to see him drop his drawers and dive in after me.

Well, no need to get ahead of myself.

6

To the End

Roman surfaced inches from me and engulfed me in a big wet hug, and swam us to the side of the pool, placing my back against the edge.

"Reach up and hang on. This time," he kissed my nose. "Don't let go."

I may or may not have moaned. I know I shivered. But regardless, I did what he asked and spread my arms out from my sides before grabbing hold of the ledge of the pool.

It felt sacrificial.

It felt sexy as hell. Like anything sexual with my man, I knew whatever he had in mind for my 'punishment' would rock my world.

And true to his nature his fingers found my core and slipped inside while I clung to the side of the pool.

That time I know for sure I moaned and let my head fall back to rest on the ledge while Roman worked two of his fingers in and out of me.

It wasn't going to take long. I was already sensitive from the previous orgasm and nothing felt better than being filled after a fantastic climax.

"Don't let go," Roman said and kissed my neck. My eyes were closed, but I nodded my compliance. "And don't cum."

My eyes flew open at the command. I started to complain when he kissed me... you know how I like... hard. Everything he was doing during this lovemaking session was hard. His voice, his body, and his technique.

"Is everything okay?" I whispered.

"I'm finally getting you all to myself. Nothing has ever been better," he said in between kisses. "Why?" His thumb joined his fingers and hit my swollen clitoris.

"Oh!" How on earth did he expect me not to let go *or* cum? "This is different." I managed to get out.

"This sweet pussy is finally going to be mine," He slowed his thrusting and went deeper than I thought he could with just a couple of fingers. I clamped down on him, signaling my impending climax. "Don't cum babe. I want to be inside of you when you cum this time."

"You better hurry!" I yelled as the first wave of my orgasm washed over me. He didn't hurry, however. He continued to thrust his fingers inside of me and kept his thumb engaged so my orgasm intensified no matter how hard I tried to hold it back. I shouted again and let it go. I mean, there was no stopping it at that point and I might as well enjoy the rush. I moaned and let my head fall back as it washed over me.

Once my orgasm subsided and I had a handle on myself, I whispered, "I'm sorry." And let my head flop forward onto his shoulder.

"I'm not sorry, Angel. You can't control yourself with me. Don't be sorry about that. I like it." His voice dropped even more. "A lot. Gives us something to work on."

"Work on?" What was he talking about?

"Yeah, you know we have the rest of our lives to go through all the ways I can make you lose control. I plan to find each and every one of them. It's going to be fun. Now wrap your legs around my hips."

I did as he asked and wrapped my legs around him without letting go of the edge of the pool. He must have been proud of me; I was finally getting my reward.

A reward was exactly what I received. I was rewarded several times that night in that pool. First, with my legs wrapped around him clinging to the edge while he thrust in and out of me. Then, on the steps of the pool, I sat in his lap, and he thrust into me.

And finally, standing up naked in our outdoor shower with one of my legs hiked up on the rock ledge. It wasn't technically in the pool but I still considered it pool play.

That beautiful man made love to me until we were both spent.

"I'm going to sleep for a bit out here. You go on in." I patted his chest to let him know it really was okay. No way I trusted my legs to get me in the door and to my bed. I was damned if I'd let that man of mine see me stumbling about. He thought I was beautiful. I needed him to keep thinking that.

I closed my eyes and leaned back against the lounger I was currently sprawled out on. I may or may not have had a silly smile plastered on my face, couldn't be sure.

I felt his arm hook under my knees and another arm tuck under my shoulders as he lifted me easily from my chosen place of slumber.

"What kind of husband would I be if I left my beautiful wife to sleep naked outdoors?" he growled.

"I'm not your wife yet." I wrapped my arms around his neck.

"You are to me."

I snuggled into his chest as he laid me in bed and climbed in after.

Bliss was the mood. Complete and utter bliss.

Would I ever get used to the knowledge that this gorgeous man was mine... and I was getting to keep him?

I fell asleep with a smile on my face.

Too bad I didn't wake up with one too.

7

Of Time

I don't know if I've mentioned this before but I'm not really what you'd call a morning person. Roman and Sophie have resigned themselves to this fact and have arranged morning activity around the house accordingly.

For one, there is always a hot cup of coffee delivered to my bedside upon my awakening. This morning it was my adopted daughter, Sophie, who delivered it. Regardless of who made the delivery, it was done the same way every time.

The cup is deposited quietly on my nightstand and the person backs out of the room as quickly and quietly as possible. No eye contact. No good morning wishes. They leave me in silence to ingest my first cup of coffee, alone. Now, to be honest, this first cup really isn't enough to get me going or make me more hospitable. It just wakes me up to a nice surly me no one wants to make the mistake of speaking to until I can get my second cup of coffee that brings me to almost human.

Almost.

The third cup is where my sparkling personality begins to emerge and I get somewhat back to normal. An early swim and shower can help to move the process along some mornings, but after the previous evening, I was tired and a little sore from all the lovemaking. Don't get me wrong, it was the best kind of sore.

I was taking my time with my first cup of coffee and thinking how amazing it would be to have a coffee bar in my bedroom like the one we'd set up for Francesca in her master suite, when Roman took his life into his own hands and broke all the rules we'd carefully constructed as a family by entering our bedroom with a muffin and chatting away like a nervous nelly.

Now to be clear, my guy was never nervous about anything. Mostly, he was the strong grunting type who handled shit and then grunted about it. It's one of the reasons I loved him so much.

But we had rules in place for a reason. The biggest reason was for their safety. I could literally kill someone pre-coffee number three. But pre-coffee number two? A suicide mission! Something big was on the horizon.

Also, he brought a muffin. It was like he didn't even know me.

I watched him with suspicious eyes as he set the offending plate down on my nightstand, right where my coffee cup normally sits mind you and smiled.

I squinted at him, may have growled... hard to tell.

"Babe, we need to talk. I don't have time for your lengthy morning ritual to prepare yourself for humanity." His voice might be sexy as heck but the words themselves were enough to make me scream.

I looked down at the half-empty cup I had resting on my chest. I had so many arguments assault my brain at once that I couldn't pin down the one I wanted to start with when he continued speaking without a care for his own life.

"We need to talk to my aunt and Aleks about the wedding."

Wedding talk before cup two? How dare he! I glared at him and went to set my coffee cup on the nightstand and realized I couldn't because the offending plated muffin was in the way.

I was preoccupied with glaring at the muffin when he said, "Having the wedding so quickly is going to be a hard sell. They are traditionalists and are going to want something to represent our Russian heritage at the wedding. There are going to be demands made."

My eyes flew to his in shock. What? I only had a few short weeks to plan a Christmas wedding and now there were going to be other requirements? This was not what we agreed on. Nor was it in the terms he'd laid out for the impending wedding criteria.

This was all Roman's fault! I needed to get rid of this coffee cup. I couldn't find anywhere to set it so I glared at Roman and spoke my first words for the day.

"Move. The. Damn. Plate."

Roman looked confused for a quick moment and then his gaze landed on the muffin. The second he lifted it from the nightstand, I set my cup down, okay to be truthful, I slammed my cup down and some coffee may or may not have splashed out. I couldn't be sure. Didn't care. I was fuming mad for so many reasons.

"See what you made me do?" I screamed. Okay, I might have cared a little. Roman's eyes looked like he was trying to hold back laughter. All that did was fuel my pre-second cup of coffee pissedoffedness.

I threw back the covers and stormed to the master bath to grab a hand towel and clean up the mess he'd just made me make. See how I did that?

"Look, I have to get going and I don't have time for your silliness."

Silliness!

That was it. I'd had enough. He had gone too far.

I stomped back to the table, wiped off the offending coffee, and threw the towel at Roman. He didn't seem as injured as I'd hoped he would be so I started looking around the room at something else I could throw at him.

"Maybe I should rile you up in the mornings more often. Watching you stomp around has just become one of my top five favorite things to watch you do naked."

Was he serious? This was no joking matter! I looked down at myself and realized I was naked, and that was in fact exactly how Roman liked me. Naked. So, I decided I'd never be naked in front of him again. Ever. That would be a perfect punishment for speaking to me before I'd finished cup of coffee number one and disregarding all the perfectly laid rules. Without saying a word, I climbed back into bed. Pulled the covers up to my neck and glared at my man.

No, it didn't have the effect on him I'd wanted, and I knew this because he smirked. But I had more tricks up my sleeve, I wasn't done with him yet. I picked up my cup and thrust it out to him indicating I needed more java. It was time for cup number two, and what was left of one was already getting cold.

This was the worst morning ever.

He took my cup, ignored my glares, and leaned over to kiss my nose before leaving the room. Hopefully, to get my second cup of coffee. As soon as he cleared the door, I wiped the kiss off my nose.

That's how mad I was.

He was right. We should tell his family about the wedding together and preferably before they heard it from someone else. Still, it didn't excuse his horrid behavior violating all the carefully laid protocols for my morning mood.

Starting my day in quiet reflection was one of the things that allowed me to operate at a high level. Even my beloved Agatha left me to my morning musings before she purred her way into my day.

Roman entered carefully carrying a giant insulated cup that I'd never seen before. It was a pretty soft teal, which by the way was my favorite color, with tiny black paw prints winding around it. The way he was carrying it made me think he'd filled it so I scooted to a sitting position being careful not to expose my chest to the disrupter.

"I was saving this for Christmas but thought it might help get me back in your good graces today. It holds almost a pot of coffee, and since it's insulated, it'll stay warm until the last drop."

"Ooohhhh." I reached for the cup with both hands. I watched him sit on the bed next to me while I sipped my glorious morning elixir.

The coffee was so hot it almost burned. Exactly how I liked it. I turned the cup around so I could look at the paw prints. I squinted closer at three that were larger than the others and had letters in them. I looked at Roman and raised my eyebrows in question.

He reached across my body to rest his hand on the bed so he was practically draped across me. Normally I liked him close, but I was still pissed. I tolerated his presence and waited impatiently for his response. He handed me his readers and I slipped them over my nose to get a better look at the letters.

"That one," he pointed at a paw print with the letters OTC, "is in memory of Old Tom Cat." The next print held a large T, "this is for Tasha. And this one is for Agatha." Tasha and Old Tom Cat were my fur babies from before. Before I'd saved Roman's life. Before I took in Sophie and she became my daughter. Before the Russian mob tried to wipe me out of existence and murdered two of my sweet fur babies while trying to get at me. Come to find out they were actually Chechens but we didn't know that at the time. They came for me because I'd not only saved Roman's life but had become an unwittingly valuable witness against them.

I looked at him with wet eyes and let my blanket slip so he could see my chest. His reward for being so thoughtful. He did love me. This was almost as good as my stunning engagement ring. I looked down at the tear-shaped diamond and sighed, it never failed to sparkle brilliantly. I moved it around on my finger with my thumb and watched it play with the light.

"I still expect a Christmas present." I took another glorious sip.

What? It's good not to leave things to chance. I *did* still expect a Christmas present.

"Okay, look. This has been loads of fun but I need to get going. Plan on dinner with my family tonight. Dress up. They're going to make a really big deal out of this."

"Of course, they're going to make a big deal out of it. It *is* a really big deal, Roman," I mumbled before I went back to sipping my almost scalding coffee. "And when they ask why we were rushing the wedding I'm telling them it's all your fault."

"We aren't rushing. You just think we are because you'd keep us engaged for years if you could." Roman picked up my hand and kissed the finger that housed the engagement ring. Then he turned my hand over and kissed my palm.

"You've given me a few weeks to plan a wedding!" I was still under the third cup level so he wasn't getting nice Sydney for a little while.

"You've had over a year to plan it." He kissed my palm again before I could snatch it away and lifted himself from the bed where he'd been sitting.

"Dress up," he said as he left the room. I watched his ass because even though he made me angry by forcing me to plan a wedding in only a few weeks, and broke all the morning rules I'd so very carefully set in place, I enjoyed the way that man looked walking away.

If I've said it once, I've said it a million times, it was the best view in the world and a bad mood was not going to change that fact.

8

To Be

I wish I could say the dinner was a lovely romantic affair that had me floating on cloud nine like any bride dreams about. But alas, no. It was an emotional nightmare fraught with all the trappings of traditional family obligations and guilt.

The night started off lovely enough, however. I was able to finish work up in time to meet the girls for wedding planning at Bellini Estate, Isabella's winery.

"Alright, I've been to the ranch and walked the area with Francesca. I think the two of us have the space where the ceremony will take place well defined. We thought it would be stunning to place a Christmas tree in the arbor and decorate it with the tree skirt and all of the ornaments we have from Raquel's wedding dress. I know it's not the same as having her here with us, but we thought it'd be a nice way to include her." Terra had her head down and her eyes glued to the notebook open in front of her. She hadn't looked up at us where we were huddled around Isabella's kitchen island. No one said anything so I didn't either. I just nodded in agreement not trusting my voice. It was times like these that made me regret staying away for so long. I'd never be able to recapture those lost years.

That meant I sure as heck was going to celebrate the here and now.

Before it got too awkward Becca said, "Wouldn't it be cool to do several wedding-style trees around the arbor too? We could hit up thrift stores and Facebook marketplace for old dresses to make skirts and ornaments."

"Jumpin' Jezebels! That's an awesome idea." Isabella's Texas drawl only surfaced once in a while. She set a platter of tasty morsels in the center of the island.

"Now, girls, these are some appetizers I've been working on. Let me know what you think."

Of course, we dove in. Before Isabella could finish explaining what she'd made they were gone. Everything my friend prepared was the best of the best and no one with any sense in their head refused her food.

"Well, I guess those will do just fine," Isabella mumbled. She picked up the empty platter and moved it to her large sink.

"I've got a lead on a horse-drawn carriage," Becca reported between chewing. "I'll text the cost when they get back to me. If it looks anything like the photos, it's adorable and will be perfect."

I nodded to Becca and turned to Jenna and removed my iPad from my oversized bag. "I have some ideas for my dress. I saved a ton of photos." I opened the file I'd made and began showing the ladies the dresses. "I like the top of this one, but the bottom of this one. And I really like the idea of faux fur cuffs and bodice with a fur muff on my head instead of a veil." I flipped through the photos pointing to the parts of each dress that I liked.

"What fabric do you want to use?" Jenna asked.

"I'm seeing winter white satin with white fur. No embellishments. Straight floor-length skirt with a slit in the front and an off-the-shoulder neckline," I answered.

"Do you want it to be fitted?"

"Yes. Simple, elegant, and classy."

"I love it. It's perfect for you."

"I know we all," Jenna looked around the island at my tribe before her eyes came back to mine, "aren't standing up with you but I still want to make our dresses match so we feel included. If you're okay with that?"

"About that." I took a deep breath. "Roman thinks you should be in the bridal party and I agree." I looked around the island again. "But it doesn't change the way I feel about having a huge wedding party at my age. It's still embarrassing."

"It's not embarrassing!" Stella yelled.

"It is to her." Terra looked at me. "What about if we all have matching dresses and we each have some kind of role during the day that establishes our motto "one for all" but we don't walk down the aisle with you?"

I sat up straight. "I like that. You girls could all sit in the front rows because you are my family anyway."

"Wait, I thought we were going to have everyone seated at the tables to watch the ceremony," Francesca said.

"I know but the more I think about it, the more I like the idea of having the ceremony separate from the reception. Is that okay and is there enough room?" I replied to Francesca.

"Of course, we have tons of room and that means fewer trees I have to find."

I smiled and reached out to her. She took my hand across the island and we held each other's gaze for a brief moment before Terra moved us along.

"Obviously, I'm planning the wedding. Becca is in charge of making sure the guests get from their cars to the ceremony. Francesca is in charge of the venue. Stella and Jules can be in charge of seating and the reception. Sloane can greet the guests, handle the sign-in and gift table, and help them to their seats. Jenna will have her hands full with the dresses and making sure everything matches. Isabella is in charge of the food." Terra licked her finger and flipped the page she'd been taking notes on.

"Becca, I liked the idea you had of wedding dress Christmas trees. Let's shoot for six of them. Jenna can make the skirts and the rest of us can make the ornaments. It'll be the coolest thing ever."

"Wait a minute," Jenna said. "There's no possible way in God's green earth I can make all of our dresses, Sydney's wedding dress, and take apart and reconstruct six wedding dress tree skirts. It's just not possible. I won't have enough time."

"Can't we just buy our dresses?" Becca replied.

Our heads swung to Becca. Not one of us said a word because we weren't sure which way Jenna was going to go with this suggestion. Normally she'd be outraged. But honestly, with the restricted time frame we were working under it wasn't a horrible idea.

"That's actually not terrible. The only drawback is finding dresses similar but not identical in matching material. With champagne, it's going to be near impossible." Jenna said.

"What about if you all wore black satin?" I said. I'd been trying to picture how the wedding photos were going to look and I was having a hard time seeing the champagne.

"Black?" Jenna asked.

"Yep, I see the photos in my head, the men in their black tuxedos, and white ties, you girls in your black dresses with white rose bouquets, and me in white carrying a red rose bouquet. Roman's tie and vest will be red to link him to me and your roses will be white to match the men's ties and vests. The flower girls in Christmas red. What do we think?"

The smiles on my friends' faces told me everything I needed to know. "One last thing. I want to have faux fur-trimmed floor-length black capes for all of you to wear too. Will that be hard Jenna?"

"No! I love the entire picture forming in my head!" She replied excitedly.

The rest of the meeting was focused on the minutiae of details. I was really getting excited and I'd never admit it to Roman, but if it weren't for his ultimatum, I'd never have planned a Christmas wedding. I was really looking forward to it now.

Now to tackle the Russian side of the family.

9

My Lawfully

It was always a formal affair with Roman's Russian aunt and uncle. Especially, with us announcing the date of our wedding and extending an invitation to them. So, it was going to be even more festive. I braced for a long night.

Luckily, I made it home before Roman. I hurried through the last bit of work I needed to complete to make sure Safe Haven was set for Christmas so I could focus on my wedding. Safe Haven was a home for human trafficked victims who couldn't go home or had no home to return to once we rescued them. It was run by the most powerful woman I knew. She ran that place with kindness and understanding... as long as you didn't cross her. Cross her and your world falls apart.

I was applying the finishing touches to my hair when I heard the shower start. Minutes later Roman appeared behind me in the mirror. He stood watching while I worked my fingers through my shoulder-length cut. I smiled at his reflection

"Safe to come in?"

I laughed at how he made sure the coast was clear before entering anytime I was in the process of my beauty routine.

"It's safe honey." I smiled.

I watched him in the mirror lean down and plant a kiss on my cheek, and step back.

"You better hurry if you're going to shower," I said.

"Just a quick rinse and I'll be ready." It must be nice to be able to jump in the shower and be ready in just a few minutes. I looked down at my plethora of lotions, potions, and perfumes and sighed. I wouldn't trade my girly girl status for anything. I loved being fancy.

True to his word in only a short amount of time Roman was back at my vanity asking for help with a cufflink. He looked amazing and smelled even better. I smiled. I felt like I was in a time warp when I was alone with him and the rest of the world faded away. I never wanted it to end.

"Are your cousins going to be there?" I asked, working on his cuff.

"I asked for everyone to attend dinner this evening."

"Do you think they know why we asked to see them?"

"Yes, but I don't think they have any idea it will be this close."

I smiled up into his face. "All done."

"You better get dressed babe or we're going to be late." I looked at my handsome man in his black tie and knew the dress I chose was going to be perfect.

"Go wait for me in the living room. I'll be out shortly."

Roman kissed my cheek for the second time since he'd been home and left me. The gown I'd chosen was one of Jenna's newest creations. It was a deep gold satin with a simple sweetheart bodice and spaghetti straps of gold chain (kind of her signature). The dress flowed low on my hips giving the illusion of a longer torso than I actually had and gave me curves where I had none. The shoes were made of the same deep gold and were a comfortable closed-toe pump with a golden chain, similar to the straps of the dress, secured around my ankles. Jenna had inserted a slit just to the left of the front of the skirt. I left my hair down and slicked it back behind my ears. Golden-hued pearl studs along with my engagement ring were the only jewelry I wore. The dress was enough. I'd applied my signature red lip with dark smokey eyes and was ready to get this evening started.

I entered the living room where Roman stood at the bar holding a whiskey tumbler. He was just about to take a sip when his eyes met mine and then dropped down to my dress. My stomach had butterflies. I could feel his eyes on me. The energy in the room shifted.

I stopped to take in his large frame, as well. He was already broad-shouldered but the crisp black jacket made him seem even wider. At that moment I saw the man he could have been. A generational Russian Mafia Boss. Roman was a good, kind hero, but no one could deny he had a sinister nature about him. It was probably why he was so good at being a cop. He knew what the bad guys were going to do before they did.

His green eyes sparkled at me. At that moment I knew if I wasn't very careful my dress was going to get wrinkled.

"Roman, let's get on the road, yeah?" I asked, not making a move. He was watching me now like a predator watching the meal for the night. Goosebumps broke out over my skin.

I loved this side of him. The dangerous side. The side he usually kept locked down tight. However, when he did let his dangerous side out it was typically around me and it usually meant a lot of orgasms. Which normally, I loved. But we didn't have time for that now.

I had to tread carefully.

"Your aunt won't be happy with us if we make them wait to serve dinner," I said, hoping that bringing up his aunt would have the same effect as bringing up a man's mother and kill the sexual tension. Roman's aunt was a fair, small, frail appearing woman with the shrewdest eyes you've ever seen. Roman says not to underestimate her. She made her way from Russia to the states and has managed to stay married to his uncle Aleks for decades. She's not only wise counsel for

Aleks but she is also the only person in the world Aleks truly fears.

That said everything about her.

I watched as he took another sip of his whiskey without taking his eyes off me. He set his tumbler down on the bar and stalked to where I waited for him.

Yes, stalked!

"Angel." His deep gravelly voice forced shivers to run over my skin. They joined the goosebumps that were still lingering. "You look gorgeous."

I couldn't help myself, I leaned toward him. It was all the invitation he needed and before I knew what he was up to he had me plastered against the wall and his mouth was descending to mine.

"No!" I yelled and turned my face away from his. He was going to smear my red lipstick all over my face. I would have to spend an hour fixing myself. Since Roman rarely did anything worth doing quickly, we were looking at a two-hour delay at least and that would not serve us. Also, it would be beyond rude.

He put his hand on my chin and forced me back to face him.

"Please," I whispered. I don't think I'd ever stopped him before so this was a new situation for us both. "I don't want to be rude to your family on the night we tell them I'm to join the family and become one of you."

Roman's thumb stroked my chin but he didn't move away. "Angel, you owe me after this." I nodded my head that I agreed with him but remained silent.

I could feel his breath on my face when he continued. "I want you in this dress, these shoes, and your hair back from your beautiful face, just like it is now when you give yourself to me."

I broke out in a sweat. The man had the sexiest voice I'd ever heard and when he said things like this it was almost impossible to think of anything other than complying with whatever he demanded.

Thankfully, he let me go. But his hands never left my body, save the trip around the car, after he put me in, and removed me from the car, once we arrived.

The ride to Aleks huge home was silent. Something was shifting in our relationship and I wasn't sure what it was. I didn't know how I felt about this new weird energy either.

Regardless of how off Roman and I were being with each other, we were met with boisterous greetings when we reached our destination.

"*Romanov* your bride is stunning as always! She is much too beautiful for the likes of you *plemyannik!*" His uncle Aleks enclosed me in a warm bear hug before passing me along to his wife, Roman's aunt Anastasia, who kissed both of my cheeks and patted my arms.

"My goodness don't you look lovely, *plemyannitsa*," she said in her small heavily accented voice. The husband and wife couldn't have looked more ill-fitted if they had tried. It was impossible to imagine them as a couple. He was a large barrel-chested beast of a man with a bald head and was covered in tattoos. He wore an old-fashioned suit and buttoned-down vest and even a pocket watch that finished off the look magnificently. Well, in a weird Russian mafia stuck in multiple time periods kind of way. His hands were tattooed, as well as each finger. The writings were in Russian so I had no idea what they were about.

Anastasia was a frail, fair woman with perfectly coiffed blonde hair with a damn taira perched on top. Her gown was a heavy lace overlay in pale pink with a straight floor-length skirt and a matching quarter-sleeved bolero jacket. She wore elegant gloves and kitten-heeled shoes. Around her neck was a stunning diamond and ruby necklace that most people would automatically think was costume but I knew better. She'd never be caught in anything that wasn't the genuine article.

I glanced back at the pair once the hugs and greetings were properly executed.

This was my new family. I looked up at my handsome fiance'. At least we'd never be bored.

10

Wedded

W e were escorted to their sitting room shortly after we arrived. Being in the Stognasfky home was like being transported back in time. Everything about the interior of the home felt like props from a movie about Mother Russia during the gilded era, if Russia even had such a thing. However, I knew better than anyone; nothing in this home was fake.

Fine gold-rimmed crystal and china. White gloved servants. A roaring fireplace that we sat in front of, in horribly uncomfortable highbacked chairs. The men drank whiskey from heavy cut tumblers and we women drank sweet liquor from tiny crystal stemmed glasses with gold rims. I looked suspiciously at the metal around the rim of the glass I was to put my lips on. I had no idea how old these were, I just hoped they were real gold and I wasn't giving myself some kind of metal poisoning.

"I love your tiara," I took a sip of the sweet delicious drink. That was the right thing to say because she literally fluttered her hand up to the top of her head and giggled.

"I know it's silly to wear it but I do love it so. If you can't wear a tiara in your own home, where can you were one?" She took a delicate sip from her glass.

I thought about that. She wasn't wrong.

"Well, now I know I can wear one here, I'll have to get one too for our family dinners." I winked at her. I thought that would be a perfect bonding thing for us. Bonus, I would get to wear a tiara. Becca was going to have a field day with this if she ever found out.

"Oh *plemyannitsa*, I have several my mother left to me, plenty for you and the girls. I'm happy to gift you one just as soon as you and *Romanov* are wed."

Now was as good a time as any. I turned my upper body towards the men.

"Roman, I'm sorry to interrupt you, but I think now might be a good time to make our announcement." Now that a vintage family heirloom tiara was being included in the deal, the night just got interesting.

"Announcement?" Aleks boomed. It was his normal voice, but the man was loud.

I rose, went to Roman, and tucked under his arm.

"Aleks," he nodded. "Anastasia, Sydney and I have decided on a date for our nuptials."

Roman's aunt and uncle looked at each other and for just a moment it seemed like they were apprehensive. I knew they liked me so I didn't understand what the look was about.

"Christmas Eve we are to be wed at the Four F Ranch. It's an evening wedding," Roman kept it short and sweet. Leave it to my guy not to drag anything out by including details.

I expected toasting and shouts of happiness. I wasn't expecting hesitation and awkwardness. But that's what we were met with. Thankfully, I was standing with Roman. I grabbed the back of his jacket. The silence in the room was unnerving. I needed to say something.

"I'm sorry if this caught you both by surprise. Roman insisted we get married right away and since I didn't want to get married in Las Vegas this was the only viable solution. Besides, it's going to be wonderful to have our anniversary on Christmas Eve." I was starting to ramble because this loud gregarious couple was silent and still.

They were totally freaking me out.

"Of course, dear, I'm so sorry for our rude behavior. Of course, we are thrilled to hear you've set a date. What can we do to help with the preparations?" Anastasia seemed to catch herself. But, something was wrong. This wasn't the level of excitement I was expecting.

"Romanov, we need to talk," Aleks said to Roman in Russian. I didn't speak fluent Russian but had begun learning the language because this would be my family. Since they weren't always above board on all things, I thought it good to know what they were saying when they thought I couldn't understand them. They didn't know I was learning Russian.

I liked it that way.

"Speak English Aleks." Roman always insisted I be in the loop. I think he knew I wouldn't just sit by when something was happening. If I didn't know something I wanted to know I'd dig. He didn't like me digging. Paused problems. Therefore, Roman liked to keep things out in the open. I appreciated that.

"You know what will happen as soon as word gets out you've picked a date." Aleks ignored Roman's request to speak in my language.

I looked up at Roman. "What will happen?"

I ignored the surprised looks Aleks and Anastasia gave me when they realized I understood what Aleks had said.

"It's nonsense and doesn't matter." Roman dismissed my request without actually addressing what the problem might be. I let go of his jacket and turned to Anastasia.

"What is going to happen that may have an influence on my wedding?" I asked her.

"Romanov needs to be the one who tells you, dear." She broke eye

contact and took a sip of her drink.

I gave Aleks a hard look and raised my eyebrows.

"*Romanov* was betrothed at his birth to the daughter of a Russian *Bratva* leader. The family has grown in Mother Russia since we left. I'm afraid they have become one of the most influential families in our ancestral region. The daughter reached the age of marriage several years ago but since *Romanov* wasn't involved in the family business, they didn't push the subject. Lydia is a very strong figure now but has remained unmarried. Now that Roman is engaged the family has pushed for her to marry *Romanov* or they will find another man for her to marry that will benefit the family." Aleks took a sip from his tumbler and went on, "she doesn't want to get married. She's been able to remain unmarried this long and prefers it. But if she has to marry, she's declared she prefers *Romanov*." Aleks took another sip. "This at least had kept her father at bay. Now he will force her to choose... or he will do it for her.

"Seriously?" I asked. I felt like I just stepped back into a time warp. "That's not cool. I didn't realize Russia was so backward." I thought for a moment. "Other than giving her Roman, and that isn't happening so don't even think about it, what can we do to help her?"

"This won't affect us, Angel," Roman said quietly.

"How can it not?" I replied.

"Because for one, arranged marriages aren't enforceable in the U.S. and second, I love you and nothing is stopping me from making you mine." Roman rested his forehead against mine. "This is an outdated tradition that is not only ridiculous but insulting to the betrothed bride."

"I agree with *Romanov*! These outdated traditions are not worth consideration. Now, I have something very special for you my beautiful, *plemyannitsa*. I've been saving it for the woman who captured our *Romanov's* heart." Anastasia rose gracefully and left the room.

"This will not go away quietly, plemyannik. No matter how hard you wish it," Aleks switched back to speaking to Roman in Russian.

"What exactly does that mean, Aleks?" I asked. "I have a wedding in full planning mode with only weeks left to pull it together. If something or someone, is going to disrupt it, I want to be ahead of the game."

Roman lifted my hand to his mouth and kissed my knuckles.

"We wed on Christmas Eve, or Christmas morning your ass is on our plane and we are exchanging our nuptials in Las Vegas. End of story. No more discussion of betrothals or wedding disruptions." He looked at Aleks. "I brought Sydney here to share our good news, and invite you and Anastasia to our wedding. I did not bring her here for you to push your manufactured obligations on us and upset my bride. I should have known you couldn't just be happy for us. You'd try to force your agenda and make this about you."

Oh Lord, Almighty! Roman rarely got this pissed. He was the calmest man I knew. I was afraid for the future relationship between these two. Aleks would never stop being who he was and Roman would never be a man to roll over and do as he was told. Much to Aleks dismay. I knew in my heart of hearts that Aleks would cross a line one day, that he wouldn't be able to step back from with Roman.

I could only hope that day happened *after* the wedding.

11

For Better

Anastasia couldn't have come back at a better time. Thankfully, it was just as Aleks' face turned red and the already uncomfortable discussion was on the verge of escalation. She entered the room with two of her three daughters, Annika and Nadia, trailing their mother carrying an old-fashioned type of hatbox. The girls were very nice, soft-spoken, and very blonde just like their mother. Since Aleks was bald I had no idea what his original hair color had been so I assumed they took their fair hair from Anastasia.

Nadia and Annika were two of the younger cousins of Roman's. So, I guess they would be my cousins soon too. I smiled to myself. I was getting a real family, along with all the dramatics and personalities that come along with being part of a family. I couldn't wait.

"Is Sophie here too?" Annika asked.

I shook my head and smiled when she asked for my adopted daughter. "No, she's at Francesca's with her daughters plotting out the wedding."

"Have you chosen a date?" Nadia asked.

I glanced at Anastasia who shook her head, "This is your news to tell, *plemyannitsa.*"

I smiled at the girls. "We've decided to have a Christmas Eve wedding."

I loved that they both screamed and jumped up and down. First, they hugged each other, and then they hugged me before turning their attention to Roman who was arguing quietly with Aleks.

I ignored the men and the girls because I was excited to see whatever it was that Anastasia had for me. She perched on the edge of one of the loveseats and patted the spot next to her. She waited until I was seated and had placed my drink on the side table before she placed the hatbox in my lap.

"This was *Romanov's* mother's veil. It was hand-made by her grandmother for her marriage to Aleks brother. It's heavy Russian lace. *Romanov's* mother's family was well known for their exquisite hand-made lace." She sighed. "Unfortunately, the family line died off and those skills were lost. To my knowledge, this is the only lace left in our family from that time." She removed the box lid and carefully lifted the lace. It was silky and not what you'd call lace by American standards. It was heavy and thick and so very soft.

It was also ivory and old fashioned. My dress was winter white and modern. I broke out in a sweat. I gingerly took the lace, leaned over, and kissed Anastaia's creased cheek. I wasn't sure what I was going to do about a veil that was drastically different from the dress but now wasn't the time to stress about it. Now was the time to be family.

"Thank you so much, *tetya*." I'd learned the Russian words for aunt and uncle just for this occasion. I was so happy I did when she broke all of her polite protocols and grabbed me up for a hug. "I'll treasure it."

"Tell us all about the wedding. What dresses are we wearing? I can't believe it's finally happening." Nadia spun, clapping her hands.

"Who is your maid of honor? Are we the bride's maids or the flower girls?" Annika asked. Shoot. I should have thought this through. I hadn't even considered the girls would want to be part of the bridal party.

"Oh silly, you're too old to be a flower girl!" Anastasia laughed.

"I'm not having any bridesmaids and I was planning to ask Sophie to stand up with me."

The looks on the girl's faces broke my heart. I had to include them. This was what family was all about. Including each other.

"What I've decided to do is have all the ladies, you girls included, wear black satin dresses. Jenna has them ordered so she'll need your sizes right away, and assign jobs. You'll be part of my wedding party and in all the pictures. I just thought I was too old to have a huge bridal party walking down the aisle or standing at the altar. I wanted it to be more intimate." I tilted my head. "Not much fanfare as far as the ceremony goes. It'll just be Roman, Sophie, and I standing at the altar. The real drama will be the decor and food. It'll be Christmas Eve so we are planning on having a feast."

"Oh, that's wonderful!" Nadia hugged me again. "What jobs are we being assigned?" I wanted them to be happy and feel included.

I had to think fast. These girls weren't going to settle for a minor job.

"I thought you could be in charge of making sure the men got their tuxes, the right tuxes, their boutonnieres, and you and your sisters will be in charge of Roman. Without the groom, there's no wedding." I smiled and was relieved when huge smiles broke out on both of their faces.

"We can totally do that!" Nadia clapped her hands again.

"I'll add all of you girls to the group text with the others who are helping to plan. You'll work directly with Jenna. And you'll need to establish a group text for the men involved as well." I tilted my head. "Where's Katrina?"

Katrina was the oldest of the three girls and the most aloof. I wasn't sure what was up with her but I knew she rarely involved herself when Roman and I visited unless she was forced to.

"*Pfft*, you know Katrina. She doesn't like being with us unless *Mama* forces her." Nadia nodded her head in agreement as Annika spoke.

"Now girls, you know our Katrina is very private. You two make it impossible for her," Anastasia admonished the girls.

"More like we make it hard for her to keep her secrets!" Nadia said with a red face.

I was catching the drift that more was afoot at the Stognafsky house. Maybe it wasn't only Roman and me that she avoided.

We spent the rest of the evening discussing the wedding plans over a romantic candlelight dinner at the formal table that could easily seat twenty people. Roman and Aleks joined in off and on but spent most of the time in silence glaring at each other over the course of the decadent meal.

Roman was unusually quiet on the way home. I placed my hand on his thigh. "What's bothering you?"

He glanced at me before turning his eyes back to the road ahead. "I don't want you to worry about it, Angel."

"Are you worried about it, Stognafsky?" I asked.

He lifted my hand from his thigh and kissed my fingers. "I won't be once I get you home and have my way with you."

I shivered.

"Okay."

12

Or Worse

That night Roman worked all his demons out on my body and it was glorious. It didn't stop me from worrying about what might be coming or if some other woman was coming to try to claim my man. I knew in my knower that Roman was mine and he wasn't going anywhere. But I still had something tugging at the back of my mind that this wasn't going away.

The next morning while I was lying in bed replaying the previous evening and sipping on the second section of my morning coffee in my amazing new insulated cup, I watched Roman flit around the room as he prepared to leave for the day.

"Your aunt gave me your mother's veil," I mumbled.

"I was there," Roman said, not looking at me.

"It doesn't match my dress."

"Then don't use it." He still wasn't looking at me. He seemed more preoccupied than normal.

"Don't you want me to use it?" I set my coffee down on the side table and scooted into a seated position in bed.

"Whatever makes you happy." Roman was distracted. If I didn't get to the root of his distraction before he left for work, I'd be distracted all dang day wondering what had him distracted!

No one wanted that.

"Honey, why don't you come sit next to me for a minute so we can chat?" I patted the bed next to my leg and scooted over a tiny bit.

"Don't have time. I'll see you tonight." He kissed the top of my head and left the room without a backward glance. Well, shoot. Maybe he hadn't worked out all the demons last night as I'd thought. Seemed there were still a couple rumbling around inside his head.

I picked up my phone and texted him a reminder that we were supposed to find a jeweler to pick out our wedding bands.

All I got back was "K"

Damn, it was worse than I thought.

I located the group text on my phone. I needed to lay out the previous evening's weirdness with Roman's family to my tribe but it was going to be way more than I wanted to text.

I decided instead to send them a voice recorded message, "we told the Russians about the wedding and come to find out Roman was betrothed to some Russian Mafia princess who now might come to America because Roman and I set a date. Also, Roman's aunt gave me his mother's gorgeous lace veil that I feel obligated to work into the wedding but it's the complete opposite of the vibe I'm going for. Oh, also, Jenna you'll need to add three more dresses to the order. His cousins want to be in the wedding. I put them in charge of Roman and the men," I said without taking a breath.

I set my phone on the bed next to me and grabbed my cup for a much-needed caffeine infusion. I was still far below my normally required amount before interacting with others, but so much was going on that I couldn't wait.

The first response was from Terra. *"Send me a photo of the veil."* She texted.

Next Jenna. *"I'll need their numbers so I can get their sizes and coordinate the men."*

Francesca; *"Breathe sister."* Accompanied by a smiley face emoji and a red heart.

Stella; *"Are we still meeting tonight?"*

Thumbs up from Jules. That meant she was probably busy in an early board meeting.

And finally Becca; *"Russian Mafia Princess! We don't have one of those yet!"* with a big eyes emoji. Leave it to Becca to find the fun in anything.

I texted back; *"Can't meet tonight. Roman and I are supposed to pick out our wedding bands."* My comment earned a bunch of hearts and smiles with heart eyes.

I took another sip of coffee and tried to figure out how I was going to get Roman to open up.

13

For Richer

I'm sad to report the wedding band shopping was less than spectacular. In fact, it was nothing. Nada. Zip. As in, it didn't happen.

Roman was supposed to be home by four that afternoon so we could head out. We'd planned to hit some of the smaller jewelers downtown so we were supporting our local small family-owned businesses.

But he never showed up. When five o'clock hit I texted him and waited for a response. When six o'clock came around I started calling him but my calls went straight to voicemail. Not like he sent them there but like his phone was off. No ring, just straight to voicemail.

By seven o'clock I'd run the gambit of being irritated, to pissed, to full outrage and plotting his demise, but quickly cycled through to fear. I was sure something had happened to him.

At eight I'd called the department and learned he'd left around noon and hadn't returned. I called the local hospital and thankfully he wasn't there.

By now I was furious.

I muttered, "he better have a damn good explanation for blowing me off." He was in law enforcement and I knew better than most how dangerous his job could be, so he may legit have something more important taking up his time.

I decided to get out of my own crazy head and took myself out for a long aggressive swim. I had no idea what time it was or how long I'd been swimming when I heard someone else in the pool with me. I surfaced to find Roman slapping out laps almost as aggressively as I had been earlier.

I swam to the edge and pulled myself up to sit while I left my legs dangling in the water. I watched him work off whatever it was that had kept him from me and buying our wedding bands. His arms slapped down on the water so loudly I was a tiny bit worried he was going to wake Sophie. She wasn't a child, but she still needed her first real home to be a safe place where she didn't have to worry about either of the parental figures in the home.

Roman continued swimming until well after midnight. At some point the concrete under my rear became uncomfortable so I got up and padded in my bare feet to the kitchen for a glass of wine. feeling awkward, I grabbed my glass and wandered to the master bedroom. Truth was, I didn't know how to gauge Roman. I'd only seen him like this a couple of times. In the past, it had been exceptionally heinous crimes that would bring out the broody alpha in him, I wasn't sure that was the case tonight. I didn't know if I wanted to see him… or avoid him.

He decided for me. I entered the bedroom as he was coming out of our bathroom with a towel around his lean hips. I stopped short and offered him my glass. He took it and drank the entire pour in one gulp before handing it back to me.

His eyes met mine. "She's coming."

I raised my brows. "Who's coming?"

"Lydia Ivanov." Roman's raspy voice was filled with disgust. He wasn't the least bit happy about this person who was coming.

"Lydia..." I was confused.

"My fucking betrothed, Sydney. For fucks sake."

What the hell?

"How am I supposed to know her name? You told me not to worry about it. She's coming? To our wedding? Or to stop it?" I asked. "And why are you mad at me?"

"Let's fly to Vegas and get married right now."

"What?" What was happening?

"Let's go tonight. We can come back and still have the wedding you and your friends are planning." His gaze pierced me.

He was clearly panicking about all of this but now he was sending me into a panic too!

But I did know one thing, and that was I didn't want to marry this man of mine in Vegas. I wanted a real wedding, complete with our friends and family, right here where our home was. The home that we were building together. It was important to me.

"I don't want to marry you in Vegas. We matter more than that." My voice held an edge of panic and I cringed.

"Where we get married doesn't matter. You and me," He gestured between the two of us, "being husband and wife is all that matters."

"It matters to me," I whispered and placed my hands on either side of his strong jaw. I could feel his muscles clenching in my palms, he was in the middle of battling some serious demons. I wished he would let me in so I could battle those bastards alongside him. I'd pick up the fight when he was weak. He needed to know he wasn't alone anymore.

"Nothing is stopping this wedding. Except you not showing up to the things I need you to be at to help me make decisions. Nothing stops this wedding." I was still irate at him ghosting me on the day we were to choose our rings. The rings symbolized the one thing he seemed to want.

Roman put his forehead against mine. His hands wrapped around my wrists and he rasped, "I'm sorry I let you down, Angel. It was a really fucking hard day."

"I know," I whispered back. And I did know. I was in it with him. I knew he had a stressful job and I respected his work. "But we still need to pick out our wedding bands."

"First thing in the morning," he grumbled and then walked me backward until my legs hit the edge of the bed. "Right now, I need you to wipe this epically fucked day away."

So that's what we did, we spent the rest of that night wiping his bad day away.

14

Or Poorer

"How can we help you?"

We'd been to three jewelers thus far. This was the last one in our small town. Whatever was going on with Roman had rubbed off on me and neither of us was feeling the joy that picking out our wedding bands should have brought us.

"Angel, just pick whatever you want." Roman squeezed the space between his eyes with his thumb and forefinger. This certainly wasn't turning out to be the romantic adventure I thought it would be. I turned to the quiet jeweler.

"We're looking for wedding bands. I'll need one to fit against this." I stuck my stunning engagement ring under the salesman's nose.

"Okay, so we're looking at white gold. This selection has several that would pair beautifully with your ring." He showed me the display case he was speaking about.

"And for you sir?" The salesman asked Roman.

"Her ring is platinum. Not gold. I just want a plain band." My head swung to Roman. This was our third store and that was the first time he'd said any of that. We really needed to work on his communication skills. I looked down at the stunning ring he'd given me, while they moved to a different case. The stone was so brilliant and large that it made sense it would be set in platinum instead of gold, but why was this the first I was hearing of it?

I abandoned the case with the dainty diamond wedding bands and joined them at the display case featuring the larger men's plain bands.

"Can you show me that one?" Roman asked, pointing to a wide plain white gold band.

I peered around his arm as he slid the band on. Chills ran over my skin.

"I have an idea," I said. The men ignored me and Roman asked how long it would take to have the wide band sized.

"I can have this back to you by the end of the week," the salesman replied.

"I've got a great idea!" I had an incredible idea forming.

"I'll take it," Roman placed both hands on the case and lowered his head. "Syd, pick your band."

Wait, did he just call me Syd?

This was not how our wedding rings were going to be chosen. Not at all.

"Look here." My voice was shaking with emotion. "First you demand we get married and I step up to please you. Then I'm sprung with the fact that some other woman thinks she has a claim on you, which I handled very well I might add, and now you're turning our ring shopping experience into a dreaded chore instead of the romantic evening it should be." My voice grew in frustration as I spoke. By the time I was done I was shrieking.

"And now, you're ignoring any input I might have about our wedding bands and you *called me Syd!*" I looked at the jeweler and worked to control my temper. "We will not be taking that ring or any other!" I turned on my heel and stormed out of the store.

Now, I didn't really think the dramatic exit through, as soon as I flung open the door, frigid air blasted my face and I realized how freaking cold it was outside. But I was already shaking mad and I couldn't stand the idea of turning around and facing him again.

He'd pushed me to my breaking point.

I stomped to the corner of the building in the opposite direction from which we'd parked, to protect my ill-clothed body from the wind, dug out my phone, and called Terra.

"How did it go?" She squealed.

Everything I'd been holding back spilled out of me. "Come get me," I sobbed.

"Babe, what's..."

"Just come get me! I'm texting you the address now, I need you to come!" I heard the door swing open and footsteps heading away. I didn't want to fight with Roman. He was in a dark mood and I was terrified if we fought at that moment we would both say things we didn't mean. Things that might change our relationship forever. Words we would never be able to get past or forget.

I knew I wanted to. I wanted to lay all of this on him. He was the one who had made the ultimatum on the wedding. He was the one who had a *betrothed* for heaven's sake! Now he was being a complete ass and I was over it. In all honesty, I wanted to battle hard with him. I was ready to explode. He was frustrating and making demands I didn't like.

But... I also loved him and did want to have him all to myself forever and ever.

I took a deep breath and reminded myself that I had to pick my battles carefully, as would he. If I was in this then I needed to remember that it was a long game. Years of battling to the death on everything, even important things, would break us both.

So, I asked myself, was this the hill I wanted to die on? The answer was a resounding no. But I certainly wasn't okay with the way he was treating me either. The work ahead would be to figure out the balance.

I stood in the alley next to the corner shivering until I heard heavy footsteps walking quickly back to the jewelry store and the door swooshed open. My stomach dropped. Roman was going to freak out if he couldn't find me.

My phone lit up the darkness and it showed Roman calling. I didn't want to talk to him but I also didn't want him to worry about my safety. I dismissed his call and sent him a text; *I'm okay. Just need some time to cool off. I'll see you at home.*

My phone lit up again just as Terra pulled up next to where I was standing. I raced to the white Mercedes and hopped in.

As we drove past the jewelry store Roman shouted, "Damn it, Sydney!"

"He sounds pissed, girl. What in the ever-lovin' heck is going on with you two?"

"Ever since we told his family about our engagement he's been different."

"What do you mean, different?"

"I can't put my finger on it but he has been a bear of a man and nothing I do that normally would soothe him, is working. In fact, it seems to make him worse."

Now that I was in the safety of my best friend I let the evening wash over me.

"I need to figure out what is going on with him and why his betrothed coming here changed so much for us."

"What? She's coming here?" Terra turned to look at me with wide eyes before turning her attention back to the road.

I nodded. "That's what he said. He isn't happy about it either."

"Of course, he isn't. Are you?" I watched her profile silently. "Family responsibilities are a burden that weighs you down. Roman finally won the woman he wants to spend the rest of his life with, after pining away for you for six years and then almost losing you. You finally agree to set a date and now a burden he never wanted any part of is threatening that. Of course, he's freaking out."

"But why take it out on me?" She wasn't wrong about any of it.

She turned back to me. "It's what married couples do for each other."

I looked forward but wasn't seeing the road ahead of us. All I could think about was this was the first conflict as an official couple and we were failing miserably.

15

In Sickness

Leaving Roman at the jeweler was a grave error on my part. Terra had taken me back to her place so I could talk out my feelings and form a plan of action based on an outcome I desired. I could work through my emotions with my friend and go back to Roman clear-headed without all the emotional stuff attached. I thought this was smart.

He didn't see it the same way.

After spending a couple of hours at Terra's, she took me home. Admittedly, it was later than I'd realized when I walked through the door.

The house was dark and silent. Sophie was off with her friends, so I wasn't worried about her, but Roman would typically be found in front of our gigantic television or out back in the pool. He wasn't at either of those places. My skin crawled when I walked into our bedroom and saw him sitting in one of our chairs with the lights off. He had a glass of whiskey resting on his knee and a half-consumed bottle sitting on the floor next to his foot.

I crossed the room and flicked on the light next to the bed, then sat down facing him.

His eyes were downcast and when he didn't look up at me my nerves frayed. This was worse than I thought. I could handle being mad at Roman but I didn't like it one bit, him being mad at me.

Except he was more than mad. He was silently furious.

I began recounting the evening in my mind looking for where I'd gone so wrong. Definitely, leaving the jewelry store was a huge mistake but he was already pissed to holy hell by then. I ran it over and over in my mind and for the life of me, I didn't think I'd done anything to cause his meanness.

"Should we postpone the wedding?" I asked softly. "Just until we can work out whatever it is that's bothering you so much?"

His head whipped up. The look he gave was one I'd never seen directed at me before.

"It's so easy for you to push me off, isn't it?" He sneered. Like, an honest-to-God lip-curling, sneer.

He never sneered at me.

"Other than leaving the jewelry store without you, what have I done to deserve this kind of treatment?" I kept my tone soft. The last thing I wanted was to escalate the situation.

His gaze pierced me. I saw the muscle in his jaw clench and relax several times before he said, "Isn't that enough?"

Instead of speaking, I shook my head no.

"What fiancé leaves her future husband standing alone and humiliated while choosing their wedding bands?" He pushed to his feet.

"You were already being mean to me. That's why I left. I didn't want to get in a big fight in front of the salesman."

"There wouldn't have been a fight if you'd just picked out your fucking wedding band!"

I stood. My eyes darted to the door and he moved between me and my escape.

"You're not running this time. You started this. You're going to stay and finish it. Now." His sexy as sin voice was mean and mad with an edge of cruelty to it. I'd never met this guy. This Roman. A man who was unmovable... and a little scary.

I sat back down and ran my hand along the comforter.

"I'm sorry I left. I see now it was a mistake. I won't do it again."

"You damn well won't."

I tilted my head and watched him. I didn't like this man at all. Maybe it was best that we knew what each other was capable of before we committed to a lifetime together.

"I don't want this," I whispered.

He reared back and slammed his glass to the floor.

"Do tell, Sydney. Please, by all means, share exactly what it is *now* that makes you so unhappy. Did you not get enough coffee? Was my wedding band, the one I was supposed to be able to pick out and wear, not fancy enough? Well? No tribe here to tell you how amazing you are? How horrible I am. What's the problem now? Tell me!" He roared and took a step toward me.

I leaned back and for the first time since meeting the big hunk I was frightened.

Of him.

He was frightening me, and the sad part was? I felt like he was doing it on purpose like he wanted me intimidated and for the life of me I couldn't figure out why. Trying to remain calm wasn't working. But, the last thing I was going to become was a shrinking violet. If this big jerk thought that was happening, he had another thought coming!

I shoved to my feet and screamed out in frustration, "You're scaring me. And the worst part is you're doing it on purpose! You're trying to intimidate me so I will... what? Cower? Do you need me to subjugate myself for you to feel big and strong? What in the actual fuck Roman? Do you even love me? Even a little?" I stepped toward him even though everything in my body wanted me to sit my rear back down and diffuse the situation. But my pride and temper were in charge now. And he'd gone one step too far. "And when in the hell did you start calling me Syd? Who is this bully you've become? Where is the man I fell in love with? 'Cause babe, right now, you ain't him."

He was so furious he clenched his fists. I made a point of looking down at them. I looked back at his face and at least he seemed to show a microexpression of embarrassment.

"What are we doing?" My hands covered my face. "I don't understand any of this. Yes, I was wrong for leaving the jeweler. I'm sorry."

That was the way Roman left me as he stomped from our room without saying another word. I continued to sob when I heard the front door slam and his big truck race out of our driveway. I remained in that position for an hour or several... I didn't know, time was elusive.

I couldn't wrap my head around how things had changed so drastically between us. This was the closest we'd ever come to actually getting married and seemed to be the closest we'd ever gotten to breaking up.

How to rewind time and make all of this stop?

I couldn't take the stillness of the house. Where was Agatha? Had she deserted me too? More like she was hiding under Sophie's bed from our fighting.

As I went in search of her, I had the overwhelming feeling I was going to need more cats.

16

In Health

The next morning, I woke up after only a couple of hours of fitful interrupted sleep.

Let's face it, I tossed and turned all damn night.

It was terrible. Roman hadn't come home... at least that I'd heard. He certainly wasn't in the bed next to me like he should have been. I felt his side, it remained undisturbed all night. I rose and dragged my weary rear to the kitchen to start my coffee, since no one was around to bring it to me. Plus, this enabled me an opportunity to peek at the sofa in the living room on the off chance that Roman had camped out there.

No such luck.

My stomach dropped. Where had he stayed?

Sophie bound in around seven that morning to shower and pack a fresh bag before bouncing back out. She was a bright spot for me. The energy she brought to the house made it a home. Honestly, I'd be lost without her. Her being able to finally live a carefree life, after all, she'd been through was such a blessing and one that drove me to provide a solid stable home that she could count on anytime she needed. I knew exactly what it felt like to have nowhere. No home. No place that was yours. Nothing. It sucks. That's why it was so important to me that no matter what, Sophie always has a place to call home and come back to.

No. Matter. What.

I wouldn't burden her with what was happening between Roman and me. There really was no need, it would just upset her. Since it was early; me being in a surly mood wasn't abnormal so I grunted my answers to her three questions.

"How are you?" She asked.

Grunt, Me.

"Roman already gone?"

Grunt, Me.

"First cup of coffee?" I could hear the smile in her voice.

Grunt, Me.

And so on... you get the picture. That was enough for her to give up and steer clear of me until she skedaddled back out the door again. It wasn't fair to use my morning mood to get my way, but dammit it was for her own good - I was afraid she'd read my emotions.

She didn't need that.

I didn't need that.

She certainly didn't want them.

Heck, I didn't even want them. I'd love to have other emotions running through my veins, like; joy, happiness, and security.

The emotions I was currently experiencing were icky and I couldn't wait to be on the other side of them.

Make no mistake, my heart was breaking. The man who'd faced me down last night was a part of the man I loved deeply. No, I hadn't seen that side of him before, but I'd seen enough of the other sides to know I didn't want to lose him. If only he would communicate what was going on in his head. It had to be something big or else he'd never let it hurt us like this.

I knew Roman loved me.

I knew it so deep in my soul that even while he was doing things that hurt me…or not saying things to keep me from being hurt… he still loved me. I knew it and felt pretty solid in it.

But… there was always a "but" wasn't there? Now there was a chink in the armor that allowed insecurities to grow and alter a person's ability to maintain a proper perspective.

And now… my own insecurities were creeping up. Was he getting tired of me? Was the fact that the wedding was really happening making him realize who I was? That he'd be stuck with me for the rest of his life? Maybe it was too much and he didn't know how to tell me. Instead, he became increasingly irritated with me. Less careful.

Maybe he was treating me so badly so I would break up with him? Maybe that's why he gave me the ridiculous wedding deadline.

I was driving myself crazy. There was no way I was going to be able to figure this out on my own, I was going to spiral out of control. I needed him to help me figure this stuff out. It wasn't just my life in jeopardy here.

I found my phone and sent Roman a short text; *Maybe we should seek counseling?*

I received a text back from him immediately; *No.*

I stared at my phone, dumbfounded. How was I supposed to navigate this? Another text came through; *The wedding moves forward as planned or not at all. I ordered my band from the jeweler and instructed him to leave the tab open for you to go back and choose yours. No more fucking around, Syd.*

Relief washed over me… followed by outrage. First, how dare he set the terms and conditions! Second, he went ahead and picked his ring without me? I wasn't the one who was being a jerk while choosing our wedding bands, he was. Why was I being punished?

This isn't what I want for us. This isn't working for me. I texted and then thought for a moment before sending: *I met your deadline and the way you repay me is to rob me of the joy of our wedding.*

I don't have time to hash this out. He texted back.

My anger shifted into overdrive. He was the one creating all this drama. Maybe he really didn't want to marry me. Maybe my fears weren't just fears... maybe they were true. Either way, this way of handling things wasn't working.

I love you. I want to be your wife, but I don't want to get married like this. I refuse to be bullied and since you've decided speaking is too hard, I'm telling you right now, over text, if we can't work this out... the wedding is off.

My phone immediately lit up; it was Roman. I hesitated before I answered.

"Hey," I said softly.

"I'm sorry, Angel." His sexy rumble washed over my senses, emotion washed over me and I relaxed.

"I don't want to rehash; I just want to know what I did to upset you so much?"

"You didn't do anything. I'm a fucking ass."

"Why?"

"Listen, go get your band. I don't care how much you spend or what it looks like, as long as you have it ready for our nuptials."

"If there are going to be any nuptials." I twisted my engagement ring. The idea of taking it off my finger hurt my heart and brought bile surging to my throat.

"If you think for one minute, I've gone through waiting six fucking years for us to be on the same continent, finally convinced you to marry me, that I'm letting this break us up...you've got it all wrong."

I let out a deep breath. I needed to be the bigger person this one time and let him off the hook.

"I want matching bands," I said in a rush, then lowered my voice,"That's what I was trying to tell you before everything went sideways in the jewelry store." I tried to keep my voice soft.

When he didn't respond my body tensed up again and the bile that had slipped back to where it belonged made a nasty resurgence.

Finally, I heard him expel a deep breath. "Angel," Roman's raspy moan pierced my core.

"Whatever you want, baby. I just want you to be my wife before something else happens to fuck it all up."

Ah. I saw what was happening. I'd postponed our wedding so many times he was worried I'd use any excuse I could to delay it again.

"I love you. I want to be your wife. That has never changed for me. Even after last night."

He let out another deep breath.

"Let the jeweler know what you want and get the rings ordered. I like the idea of our bands matching. If you like, you can order the same one I chose but have them make it in platinum for you… just tell them they'd better make sure it arrives in time for the ceremony."

"Okay, now, tell me what's really going on."

He let out another deep sigh. "Lydia…she's coming to disrupt the wedding. She's risen in her family's business and insists she'll lose face if I choose another over her. She's even promised retaliation if I don't hold up our ridiculous family arrangement."

"Are you serious?" Some other woman was coming to disrupt our wedding ceremony? I didn't *think* so! Wait until the girls heard about this!

"I've been arguing with her and Aleks, and if that wasn't enough of a pain in my ass, her fucking father inserted himself. I don't know why he got involved, or what he thinks he can do. It's a fucking mess."

"Isn't he like a big mafia guy? Are we in danger?"

"I'm working hard to make sure that doesn't happen. This is why I wanted no part of my family or any of their bullshit backward traditions."

"That's not reasonable. Family is family." Roman had been estranged from his uncle, aunt, and cousins for the six years after I'd saved his life. When I got back, Aleks kidnapped me so we could meet and that started things back up between them. "Why didn't you tell me when all of this was going on?"

"I'd started to, but you were so excited about the wedding plans and the girls helping you… I just didn't have the heart to ruin it for you and your friends. But, it seems I'm an asshole and did it anyway."

"Will your uncle help?" I asked.

"I'm meeting him directly after work. I'll be home as soon as we've had a chance to chat."

"Your aunt will convince him to help."

"I hope so, knowing Aleks he will try to use this to recruit her into his family."

"No. She can't live here." I was going to have to have a talk with Aleks myself before he got any ideas about bringing her here permanently.

"I don't want her here."

"What's she look like?"

"What?"

"What's she look like? I want to know who I'm wishing has a face full of acne and greasy hair!"

"Angel."

Lord Almighty!

"Don't you Angel me now after calling me Syd all damn night! You tell her to bring it! There is no way on this tortured planet I'm letting some high and mighty Russian Mafia Princess come all the way to *my* home and steal *my* man!"

Soft laughter came over the line. "Babe."

"Don't babe me."

"Angel, she's *Bratva*; a mafia princess sure, but she's also a ruthless Russian assassin. She isn't to be trifled with by you or any of your posse. I know you think you're badasses but she is a brutal killer who wouldn't hesitate to take one of you out, and then sit down to a nice steak dinner without a care in the world. You want that on your conscience?"

No. No, I did not. I loved my girls. I'd never put them in harm's way.

"I'll have to figure out a way to tell them without alarming them. We'll set up top-notch security. I'll call Lucas and get him involved."

"I've already got Cabe on the job."

Whew. Cabe was good. I relaxed a little.

"That's good. Cabe will take care of everything."

"I'm counting on it."

"We all are. And he needs to do it before Becca finds out about this. She won't stand down, no matter what we say."

"Keep them focused on the wedding planning. You are up against a deadline after all."

I knew he was trying to be playful but it felt like swallowing a bitter pill to discuss wedding plans after the discussion we just had.

"Like I said, I'll keep them as preoccupied as I can but if one of them catches even a whiff of this… there won't be anything I can do to stop the wildfire that will ensue." He must have known how right I was because I heard him growl, "Goddammit." Before he hung up.

I spent the next few weeks keeping the girls so focused on the wedding I'd begun to believe I'd managed to keep it from them.

Almost.

17

From This Moment

The wine cork garlands were a favorite with our group. We'd string them with red wooden beads at Christmas. They really added to the festivities, plus, how on brand with our group could we be? Using them in the wedding was a stroke of genius on a couple of fronts. First, I loved how they looked, we even decided that the natural element of the corks were perfect against all of the glam and glitz we were bringing to the wedding. We decided not only to string them with pearls and crystals, but we also hot glued them to the square bases of the Christmas trees.

Francesca, her daughters Faith, and Fallon, and their neighbor Luce (her name is Lucinda but if she liked you, she'd let you call her Luce) offered to run around the wine-tasting rooms and gather as many discarded corks as they could find. They'd be used, slightly misshapen, and maybe a tiny bit discolored. In other words, perfectly imperfect.

"How many do we need?" Luce was seated in the passenger seat.

"Terra asked for at least three hundred so I figure we will have to hit a couple of tasting rooms."

"It's almost Christmas! They may have all been gathered up," Luce mumbled.

"Fingers crossed," Francesca mumbled back.

Francesca cruised her suburban in front of her friend Stella's place Unpoured, looking for a parking spot. The place was packed with happy shoppers and people milling about. She slammed on her brakes when a gal lost her footing and stumbled into the road while digging through her purse, head down.

"Mom!" Faith screamed.

Francesca flexed her shoulders. Her youngest daughter screamed virtually everything...every day. She'd had her daughter's ears checked when she first started, but everything was fine.

Regardless, half of the words the child spoke were ear-piercing. Fallon was more tolerant and seemed to think she'd grow out of it. It would cause Laird's eyes to roll back into his head so there was that little bit of fun. Francesca was convinced they'd all come out of this phase of Faith's development a little hard of hearing. Ah, the price one paid for child-rearing.

"Please stop screaming." Francesca rolled her eyes at her daughter in the rearview. "All eyes peeled for a parking spot."

"Look, right there. Those people are leaving," Luce pointed at a little red convertible bug with a license plate that read "EW BUG" backing out. Francesca raced around and pulled in behind just as the little cutie was pulling away from the curb.

"Nice spot." Francesca smiled at Luce. "Everyone bale, we've got wine corks to beg for!"

Downtown Harmony Grove was a sweet historical tourist attraction made up of cobblestone streets and brick three story buildings. The street lamps were old Victorian black iron replicas, and the doors to the buildings were mostly iron and heavy mission-style wood. The cypress lined streets looked incredible this time of year wrapped in white lights, and topped with giant red bows. The bridges in to, and out of the town, were decorated with perfectly matched green wreaths and bright red bows similar to the ones atop the cypress trees. The downtown association had managed to erect an open-air ice skating rink next to where pictures could be taken with Santa. The area was bustling with people, young and old.

"Looks great down here, doesn't it?" Francesca watched a father help his two little girls try to ice skate, and smiled to herself. The four Fs had some really great years before Frank got sick. She looked back at her girls. They still had a lot of years left that were going to need happiness and maybe even a little greatness. The last few years had been all about death and survival.

Maybe it really was time to start living again.

Fuck it, she thought.

"Hey, let's hit up Stella for the corks and then go slip and slide on the ice before we take photos with Santa."

"Yes!" Fallon yelled.

"Sounds good to me." Luce didn't need to be asked twice.

"Faith? What say you, mighty shrieker?" Francesca twisted to look at her daughter and found tears running down her cheeks. She followed her line of sight and saw she was watching the same father playing with his two little girls ... as she had been only moments before.

"Oh, baby. What's going on?" Francesca took Faith's hand.

"The last time we ice skated was with daddy," Faith replied in the smallest voice she could manage.

"I know, baby. And it's good that we have those memories. I was just remembering them too. But we need to keep making memories. New ones to add to the old. That's how we keep them alive. You know you'll see your dad again many many decades from now, and you need stories to tell him of all the things you did while he was waiting for you." She didn't know if that was the right thing to say or not. Since she was struggling with all sorts of guilt, remorse, and insecurity at devastating levels of her own, it felt impossible to know what was right for her girls.

In an attempt to help her daughters, and herself, she'd set up grief counselors for the three of them. Separate or together, whatever they needed. Nonetheless, her words were what she believed and she drew comfort from them. She could only hope that the grief counselors agreed in their next session.

It seemed to make sense to the girl at the moment who immediately shifted gears by screaming, "Hot chocolate!"

Francesca gave Lucinda a watery smile and the females barreled out of the large vehicle. Strolling to Unpoured the foursome passed two boys sitting at a table filled with piles of Christmas cards.

Faith tugged Francesca's jacket.

"What's that mommy?"

The two dark-haired beauties stopped at the table.

"Want to send a Christmas Card to someone who has to live in a hospital?"

"Living in a hospital?" Francesca picked up a flyer from the table.

Adopt a Grandparent, it said. A local youth church group trying to make sure every senior citizen living in assisted living centers got at least one card for Christmas.

"We charge a dollar and that money goes to Safe Haven the animal shelter over on Sargent Road," the smaller boy rushed out.

"What about postage?"

"Naw, my mom drives us over and we deliver them to the old folks' home... I mean the hospital. We take candy canes and it makes them really happy." The smaller boy was bouncing in his seat creating a rhythm with his words.

"It's chilly, you boys okay sitting out here?"

"Yes, ma'am," the bouncing boy replied. "Our momma is over at the Second Hand Lily and ... look, she can see us out the window." He waved enthusiastically. "Also, she loaded us up with a thermos of hot cocoa and made us wear thick socks even though I didn't want to and now my feet are sweaty."

Francesca smiled at the boy. Faith picked up one of the cards that had a white snowman made of fluffy material and a red glitter scarf. "I'll take twenty." She said to the older, mostly silent boy. "Faith, baby, help me fill them out, yeah?"

"Can I do this one?" She held up the card she'd been fondling.

"Of course, baby."

They spent the time needed and scrawled sweet quotes and kind words for the recipients before hurrying into the bustling tasting room.

Faith headed straight to the back. She'd grown up surrounded by wineries and this bar specifically and knew the rules. Stella set up a cute little hang-out area with a tv and tablet for kids when they visited. The girls had been so good about heading to the back that Francesca hadn't been back there since Frank first got sick. The last thing you did was hang out at wine bars when your husband was at home with a terminal cancer diagnosis.

Francesca was impressed with the space. "Stella really jazzed this kid's area up." She'd put in a snack machine and mini fridge filled with juice and water. It was so cute and colorful, with a long blue couch, giant tv, play center, a full shelf of board games, and bean bag chairs no adult in their right mind would sit in for fear of not being able to get back up. It was just perfect for the kids.

Francesca left her daughters and Luce and went in search of the manager.

"Hey Lars, Stella sent us to retrieve whatever corks you might have." Lars was delivering a flight of whites when she found him at a round-top table built from an old used wine barrel. The ceilings were at least twenty feet high, and made of a decorative stamped tin. The walls were the same old chipped brick as outside. Lars placed the flight on the table. "We got you girl, follow me around back."

"You guys are jamming!" Francesca followed Lars to the back of the building.

"It's always packed around Christmas but now that we have the entire downtown opened up and decorated it's been a nonstop party. We're lovin' it!" Lars stopped short in front of several black garbage bags. "Here ya go."

Francesca took in the bags that were piled higher than she was. "These are filled with corks?"

"Yep. And You're gonna need help because I can't leave, not even for a second. Stella said you needed as many as we could save..." Lars motioned to the pile of full bags. "This is what we saved."

"Okay, first, thank you. But, stop saving them. This is way more than we need."

Lars dropped his head and put his hands on his hips.

Francesca rushed on, "But don't worry. We'll use them for other community events."

Lars' hands dropped from his hips and he visibly relaxed.

Francesca patted his arm. "You need a vacation, my friend."

"You're telling me!" He released a sigh. "After the holiday's things will slow down."

Francesca shook her head. After the last few years one thing Francesca felt sure about... and that was that life rarely settled down. You had to enjoy the peaceful times while you had them because chaos was the order at hand and always right around the corner; plotting, planning, and waiting for the best time to hit and knock you off your feet.

Lars elicited help from a few able-bodied patrons who were more than happy to assist the stunning brunette. Once the corks were packed away in the SUV, and after declining several invitations for wine, the four females headed out to enjoy the downtown festivities. The foursome ice skated until Lucinda fell one too many times. Francesca and her girls were worried she was going to hurt herself. They knew better than to try and convince Lucinda that her falls were going to leave her black and blue, instead the three conspired, and eventually, Fallon faked boredom so that the four together decided the next order of business was hot apple cider and left the ice rink. It wasn't too cold out. Snow and frozen ponds were a thing of fairy tales in this wine country climate, so the skating rink was a really nice treat for the girls, big and little.

Luce sipped her hot cider and moaned. "This tastes almost as good as mine."

Francesca smiled. "Almost." Lucinda was well known for her cooking abilities. Where Isabella was a baker of the highest caliber, Lucinda was a down-home, comfort food style, old-fashioned cook. She didn't know how to make as many fancy dishes as Isabella, nor did she know (or want to) how to efficiently provide five-star courses for hundreds of people... but the woman was a damn fine cook regardless, and her Davidson was one happy man. Francesca thought it was one of the sweetest things in the world when a man loved his wife's food over all others. There is something basic about it, simple and wholesome.

As if Francesca had manifested him, Lucinda's phone dinged. Davidson asking if she was ever going to come home.

"It's getting close to dinner time and I've had a couple of chickens roasting in the oven. The smell must be driving him crazy." Luce snickered. That's when Francesca saw her elderly neighbor clearer than ever before. She knew good and well that food would drive her Davidson mad and demand her return. Luce saw the look on Francesca's face. Then she noted that it was mirrored on the two younger girls' faces as well.

"What? I have to use what I have left. Once the old caboose starts dragging a gal has to have a backup plan to keep her man interested." She shook her head. "He does love my cooking."

Francesca leaned down to her daughters and stage whispered, "Davidson loves Luce regardless. Her food could taste like cardboard and that man would eat it and declare it the finest in the land." The girls snickered at their mother's dramatics. Luce pretended to be huffy and the group headed toward the Suburban.

"Now it feels like Christmas," Faith said at a perfectly respectable volume.

Francesca felt chills rush over her skin. "Has it not felt like Christmas, sissy?"

"Not really," she mumbled.

The girls hadn't been sheltered from the last five years as she'd hoped. But... of course, they hadn't been. Who was going to be the one doing the sheltering? Certainly not Francesca. She'd been too busy taking care of Frank while he was dying. First, there was hope that he could beat the cancer. Then, it became about keeping him comfortable and before she knew it, that was all that had mattered.

"Is it okay that Christmas Eve is going to be spent with everyone?" Francesca thought Sydney and Roman's wedding would be a perfect way to be distracted. After all, it was their first Christmas, without the girls' father. But maybe she was making a mistake. Maybe they needed peace and the space to celebrate old traditions instead.

Damn. Motherhood was hard.

"I'm excited about the wedding. Especially my dress. Jenna found the most beautifulest dress for me and mine is going to look almost as good as Sydney's. Jenna says no one can look as good as Sydney at her wedding because we are her sisters, and it's our job to make sure she shines. If one of us shines brighter... that means we aren't doing our job." Faith continued rambling without stopping until they dropped Lucinda off at her home across the street from the 4 F Ranch.

"Bye Luce!" Faith screamed. Well, they'd had most of the evening with her speaking at a tolerable level. It was good to count your blessings.

Francesca offered Luce a side smirk. Luce rolled her eyes and shouted her goodbyes before closing the door.

"Who is up for tacos and NCIS?"

"Me. But can we watch Polar Express?" Faith asked.

"No Polar Express!" Fallon yelled. "We've watched it a million times!"

"No, we haven't"

"Yes, we have."

"Tacos and NCIS for Fallon. Faith you can watch Polar Express on the iPad with earbuds or in my room."

Francesca turned the large SUV onto the road that came directly before a large wooden sign that read "4 F Ranch".

"It's time to change the name of our home." Fallon had not said much about how she was feeling. Francesca had relinquished the reins to the grief counselors believing it to be the best way to help her oldest daughter, Fallon, heal.

But just mentioning another big change that would be another step toward their future... and away from their past with the girls' father, was more than sweet Faith could bear. The ice skating, Christmas cards, and photos with Santa were wiped away in a flash.

The first scream was the most gut wrenching. The sobbing and screaming that came after were almost too painful for the girls' mother to bear.

Francesca stopped in the driveway and tried to calm her daughter, to no avail. She ended up racing the large vehicle up the driveway and skidding to stop just in front of their front door.

Getting Faith out of the car was another twenty minutes of pleading, begging, and bargaining. Francesca took a step back before her frustration had her physically pull Faith from the SUV and force the child into the house. In the end, Francesca was forced to call in reinforcements to help with her youngest daughter.

Thirty minutes later Francesca opened the door to one of the most beautiful faces she could ever remember seeing.

"Thank God you're here. She is inconsolable." Steve and Allistor were a husband-husband team that owned a B&B down the road. They had also taken up the mantle of a permanent fixture in the girls' lives. But Faith and Allistor had a relationship that transcended the years that separated them. He held the magic key to her emotional stability. The two of them had become thick as thieves. Allistor was the kindest, most ethical man Francesca had ever known, and loved that her daughter got to have this incredibly special relationship.

"What set her off?"

"Well, we actually had a nice evening. She'd said it finally felt like Christmas… and then Fallon suggested we change the name of the ranch, and all the good that our evening had brought vanished."

Oh, honey," Steve said.

Allistor eyes grew stormy but he remained quiet as he pushed past Francesca to seek out his girl Faith, and perform the miracle her mother had requested.

Fix her.

18

To the Next

After the latest discussion I had with Roman I decided the best course of action was to throw myself into the wedding. The two of us were going to be fine. We had to be. No other outcome was acceptable.

Now that I knew why he'd been such a bear. Note to future wifey self; when hubby acts like a giant jerk; something big is going on - dig deeper. I made the check motion with a flick of my wrist and nodded my head. I foreshadowed that many such internal conversations would take place over the next few decades so I might as well get acquainted with the new inner wife dialogue.

Becca texted each one of us *"bitches"* that she'd *"scored the big one"* and demanded that we meet her *"pronto bravo"* at Jenna's gorgeous Tudor style home.

God bless Becca, her timing was impeccable and exactly what the doctor ordered. Dressed in a soft sage microfiber tunic with black leggings, I scooped up my sweet little orange tabby, Agatha, and pulled on my black rubber rain boots, before we trotted out to the Range Rover.

I arrived at Jenna's security gate noting the shiny black sedan parked across the street. I entered the code we'd been given, due to an insanely evil hacker who seemed to have focused his attention on my friends. We each had to secure our places and were assigned our own access codes to each other's homes. This way Cabe could track those who had been targeted if someone disappeared. Since none of us wanted to disappear, we agreed to most of his security suggestions. And since Roman was as security conscious as Cabe, my man supported the effort as well.

I pulled onto her horseshoe-shaped driveway and parked behind Terra's gleaming white roadster Mercedes. Luckily, most of us lived within only a few minutes of each other. After spending so many years away from these women I couldn't dream of ever residing a great distance from them again.

Becca's colorful beat-up truck skidded to a stop disrupting a layer of dirt that settled elegantly over my clean Range Rover and Terra's white Mercedes.

I smirked. "Terra is going to have your ass!"

"Why? What'd I do?" Becca slammed her heavy door shut and rounded the tail of the truck only to jump up into the bed itself before she began chucking several large garbage bags to the ground.

"I'd ask if you need help but those look heavy." I squinted at the bags as another landed on the cobblestone at my feet.

"They aren't heavy, they just look that way. Grab a couple and hall ass into Jenna's sewing room."

"I'm not carrying those! They're all dusty. I don't do manual labor." I shifted Agatha's carrier and stuck my nose in the air.

"Alrighty then, I'll just take these wedding dresses right back where I bought them from because *someone* has all the time in the world to go shopping for the wedding dresses Jenna needs to take apart to make *someone's* Bridal Christmas trees for *someone's* wedding." Becca jumped out of the bed of her truck and grabbed a bag. "Jenna is going to have an aneurysm!" She tossed the bag back into the bed and looked me dead in the eye. "I'm telling too."

"Wait!" I didn't know if I had a hot flash or my life flashed, but one thing I did know as well as I knew my own name, the last place I wanted to be was on Jenna's bad side. If she found out I'd sent back the dresses she'd been waiting for… I'd be the worst-dressed sister forever more and that was not a label I was willing to wear…ever.

"I'll grab a bag and tell the others to come help." I snatched one of the smaller bags and found that it was indeed much lighter than the size of the bag would have me believe. Giving Becca a squinty look I asked, "What's in here?"

"Terra and Jenna asked for wedding dresses to make wedding Christmas trees and I scored a goldmine at Second Hand Lily!" The store was one of the best around. Treasures new and old filled every nook and cranny of the bricked triple-story consignment store.

The two of us rushed the bags in as quickly as we could and found Terra, Jules, and Stella were already working with Jenna deconstructing another vintage wedding dress. Jenna had several boxes of clear multi-shaped glass ornaments scattered about awaiting adornment and hot glue gun stations set up around the room.

I plopped the bag down and set Agatha's carrier on the floor before hightailing back out to Becca's truck where the other bags were waiting. Terra rushed up behind me and slid her arm around my waist.

"How are the plans coming? Things settling down any?" She was whispering so I felt pretty confident that she'd kept Roman and my argument to herself.

"Things have settled down some," I whispered. "I learned that Roman had already been betrothed to another." I shook my head. "And like some bad spy novel, she's coming to claim her man."

I thought I was whispering but when Becca screamed behind me I realized I hadn't been quiet enough.

"Who in the fuck does she think she's messing with?" Becca was red in the face and her curly hair was beginning to frizz a bit. You could mostly check Becca's mood by her hair.

If it was tied back, she was hard at work and had no time for foolery. You were going to get short clipped answers to your questions. If it was up in a messy bun, she'd have had a long day and was probably a couple of glasses deep into a bottle of wine. This was when she was the quietest and you'd be able to get a word in edgewise. Down and curly, she was having a nice day and planning to be with her girls (us). Anytime we were together - and weren't getting shot at or kidnapped - we were having a good time. But when her hair began to go frizzy, that meant that mean-ass Becca was about to show up and kick butt like no one has ever seen and the world had better just stand down. She was small and pretty and that had fooled many unsuspecting transgressors who underestimated the epic mess of her entire being.

"Becca, keep your voice down!" I admonished. "I don't want to freak the others out."

"Fuck that!" She grabbed up a bag in each hand and marched past Terra and I. We watched her stomp her way back toward Jenna's workroom.

"Your privacy is over now. We'd better hurry back before she riles the rest of them up and we lose all of the day's productivity." Terra snatched up two bags in one hand and two in the other. I grabbed the final three and hurried back hot on her heels.

"I say we hunt the bitch down and show her no one messes with our Sydney!" Becca was really on a roll by the time we entered the shop with the rest of the dresses.

"Becca, Roman is handling it. If I'd wanted everyone upset, I would have told them myself!" Becca loved us more than she loved herself. There was something sad about the level at which she'd fight for us... and the rescues she cared for... yet, for herself, she took little care.

She drove an old beaten-up pickup truck and rarely bought herself anything. We discovered that when Francesca had talked our group into going out to Becca's ranch for dinner. She didn't even have enough plates for us to eat on. We'd chosen to eat outdoors because it was so beautiful and she had a gorgeous outdoor eating area, but when we went inside to use the restroom and to help clean up, we noticed that she had very little in the way of furniture and what she did have was utilitarian at best.

Ugly, is what Terra had called it.

That was right before the two of them got into a giant fight. Becca took great offense at Terra calling her home ugly. Terra was upset to find one of her dearest friends was living in a manner Terra felt was beneath her. Then Terra, teared up and asked if Becca even knew how much she loved her before laying on one of the finest guilt trips I'd ever heard.

And it was working until Terra made the fatal mistake of making it about herself.

"Even Sydney let me help make her home nice. Why won't you let me do that for you? Don't you trust me?"

This comment and follow-up question made Becca even madder and she eventually kicked everyone out of her home vowing never to invite us "ungrateful bitches" back again.

Then the two of them argued about how Becca should have told us how she was living. That's when Becca really got offended and kicked us all off of her property. She was mid-rant but stopped herself to amend, "Francesca can come back any time she likes!" Before slamming the door.

Terra, of course, was horrified that Becca responded the way that she did. Becca was always giving one of us grief about something or other but until that moment not one of us had realized how sensitive she was about her place. The rest of us were used to Terra offering to help with our homes… I guess we just got used to it.

It took Cabe finally getting so sick of Isabella complaining about how the tribe had fractured (plus she stopped baking because she was too upset) that he went to Becca, put her in his truck, and dropped her in front of Terra's home with clear instructions to "fix this fucking shit" before he sped off. No one but them knew what was said but they did indeed "fix it" as Cabe had instructed.

The tribe was mostly back to ourselves and Isabella was back to baking for her husband. All was right with the world.

"Becca, what the hell did you buy?" Jenna asked.

"What do you mean 'what did I buy'? Wedding fucking dresses, girl" She shook the one she was pulling out of the bag. "Can't you see?"

"Well," Jenna pulled a frilly mess from the bag she was holding. "You were instructed to buy," Jenna used her fingers to make air quotes. "Gaudy beaded wedding dresses with long trains!" She shook the dress she was holding again. "There isn't a bead or rhinestone on this one!"

She went to another bag and ripped it open and shook it at Becca. "Or this one!"

Jenna dropped the offending garment. "Are the rest of them like these two?"

"I don't know! I saw wedding dresses for a hundred bucks each and bought them all."

"You paid a hundred dollars for this?" Jenna's eyes were wide and her mouth had fallen open.

Becca nodded affirmatively but didn't move or say anything further. The rest of the girls stopped moving and waited for whatever Jenna would do next.

"Okay, this is what we have. I need to figure out what we can use and what we need. This changes everything."

"How can this change everything? You asked for wedding dresses and here they are. Geez. Try to be helpful and this is how you're treated,"

Becca mumbled and began shoving the dress she was holding back into the bag. "I'll take them all back!"

"Terra, you go with Becca and see if they have any heavily beaded dresses with long trains."

Terra's eyes grew wide. She looked around the room for an escape but found none.

Jenna caught a look. "You and Becca need to figure this out. We don't have time for anything but efficiency. And if for some reason you can't find dresses with beading, get the dresses and then go to the craft store and purchase lace appliqués, pearls, and rhinestones."

Since this was mostly my drama and I was super happy that the conversation shifted from me and Roman to Becca and her bags of crappy wedding dresses I offered, "I can go too."

"No, you're trying on your actual wedding dress." Jenna picked up Agatha's carrier and moved her into the adjoining room where the walls were lined with sample clothes. She set the carrier down and cooed to Agatha, "Would you like some tuna sweet girl?"

One thing you could always count on with our sisterhood, we always, and I mean always, spoiled each other's pets. It was an unwritten rule that we followed the letter of the unwritten word.

"Bumble doesn't like to share, but what she doesn't know won't hurt her," Jenna continued.

I turned my attention to the platform that was surrounded on three sides by mirrors. On the mannequin was a stunning sleek winter white sheath of a dress. There weren't any sleeves, the skirt fell straight and gathered on the ground, and the train was only pinned to it... but it took my breath away.

Chills ran up and down my arms. This sleek white vision was my dress. I felt it in my bones. She was gorgeous. I pinched a small amount between my thumb and forefinger, the fabric was thick, soft and buttery. I looked at the large gathered yards she had draped around and pinned to the back of the dress and my eyes grew wet. It was so much more than I could have dreamed on my own.

I felt all the love Jenna had wrapped up in this incredible dress and the last thing I was going to do was let anyone screw it up.

19

For Ever More

On the second attempt, we managed to get the perfect bridal dresses to repurpose once Becca and Terra came back from exchanging the rejected ones at the Second Hand Lily. Seems Becca had skipped over the plethora of beaded rhinestone encrusted dresses for the fluffy frilly ones... because she just didn't know. Becca couldn't see the vision the other girls had so to her the bigger the better. Once Terra pointed out what they were looking for, a light bulb must have clicked because she was a dog on a bone afterward. The twosome arrived back lickety-split and we set up the operation in what started as an efficient assembly line but quickly dissolved into organized chaos as soon as the margaritas started flowing.

The chaos began when Jenna removed the wedding dress trains to make the tree skirts, then passed them to Jules.

Becca yelled, "Drink up, my bitches!" Of course, we did because... margaritas.

Jules removed the pearls, crystals, and rhinestones and then passed what was left of the dress to Stella who carefully unstitched the lace and appliqué... and Becca yelled, "Drink up, bitches!" You get the idea. At every handoff there was a drink required... pretty soon we were on our way.

The deconstructed items were handed off to me, Becca, and Stella. and we proceeded to hot glue lace, pearls, and crystals to the clear glass Christmas ornaments. The results were quite stunning and we were excited to decorate the trees. We used white satin hangers that finished the ornaments off beautifully.

At some point, music was introduced and before I knew it Stella was cueing up a playlist she and Jules had assembled of the world's sappiest love songs. That only lasted through three songs before Terra took the reins, and synced her favorite playlist which began with the Guardians of the Galaxy soundtrack from movie one.

Now the party was in full swing and we were laughing, dancing, and drinking our way through the wedding dresses.

After that, we worked on stringing large faux pearls, with wine corks that Francesca's neighbor Davidson had drilled through the center to accommodate the string. We'd collected about five thousand not realizing how eager the local wineries were to get rid of them. We chose to drill and string one thousand corks and leave the rest for future projects.

We were so close to the wedding that I was worried we wouldn't get everything completed in time but why I even wasted any time stressing about that was beyond me. My girls would never let me down. They could and would move mountains for me... I knew this because I would do the same for them.

It took several days but we finally had twenty-six wedding dress tree skirts (including Raquel's that was on loan from Isabella) and matching ornaments. The pearl and cork garlands turned out so nice that we decided to add crystal to the pearl and cork, as well. The effect was classically whimsical, and perfect for us.

Perfect for my wedding....

Lord Almighty! I meant my and Roman's wedding. When was I going to get this straight? I shook my head. I hadn't heard from him for quite a while and he wasn't checking in with me like he had been. Two nights earlier he'd worked through the night and only came home to shower and head back.

Now in all honesty, on massive cases, he worked around the clock. I understood how important his work was. Lives depended on him and if it were me or one of my loved ones and we were counting on our law enforcement to save us... or to stop someone committing heinous crimes, I'd want Roman on my case. He was dedicated and driven. In today's climate, we needed more people with that level of dedication. The bad guys didn't take the night off, they didn't stop for lunch breaks, and they sure as heck didn't care if it was after hours. Criminals worked all hours of the day and night... the good guys needed to as well.

I understood that. It was one of the reasons I loved him so much... he was a bonafide white hat wearer. With zero shades of gray.

He lived by a strict code of conduct and he didn't sway from it. It was trustworthy and solid and I depended on his steadfastness to get us through when times were tough. Not seeing him was not unusual - but not hearing from him was.

I called his cell and left a message. Then followed up with a text and just on the off chance I might catch him, I called the station and left a message with the receptionist to call me as soon as he checked in. That was all I could do for now. He'd get back to me when he could.

I told myself once more that I needed to trust the man that he was. I knew him and knew only really big things kept him from me. We had this thing, the two of us. This incredible bond. And if I trusted it instead of second-guessing it, we would be happier.

I released a deep sigh and relaxed my shoulders. The stress was only going to increase until I walked down the aisle. If I didn't pace myself, I wasn't going to make it to the end. I'd stroke out for sure at the rate I was going. I needed to back off. I'd give him some space and trust that things were as he said and move forward with the excitement of the wedding.

The tribe was gathered at Bellini Estate for the food and cake tasting. Isabella had set aside the late morning for us girls so we could have the winery to ourselves and Isabella's sole focus. We decided the men would like anything Isabella made regardless of what it was, therefore the groom and groomsmen didn't need to worry about the tasting. Even though this was the one thing my groom might have liked to have a say on, it was one less thing to argue or stress with him over. I'd had enough fighting and I was starting to feel we might have dodged a bullet. The wedding planning was so stressful, him being preoccupied was possibly a blessing in disguise.

Plus, this way the men wouldn't have to fight Cabe for every crumb. The man could be ruthless when it came to most things but nothing touched his level of villainy when it came to anything regarding his two tiny females, his wife, or her cooking.

He was absolutely cutthroat when it came to her food.

Yes, it was delicious and honestly, the idea of Isabella cooking for another wedding party besides mine did elevate my level of possessiveness when it came to her and her skill and talent in the kitchen. Therefore, I completely understood where he was coming from. However, this didn't mean I had the time or brain space to be on the receiving end of it.

Becca was the last to arrive. Everyone who could come had made it on time but her. Which was unusual because she was a stickler for being on time. Stella, Jenna, Terra, Sloane, and I were gathered around the large island in Isabella's commercial kitchen. She had a staggering amount of food laid out in small bite-sized servings.

"What the hell?" Becca shouted after she'd set her things down and joined the others at the island. "I didn't eat dinner last night or breakfast this morning to make room for today and…" She pointed at the food displayed. "*This* is all we get?"

"Becca!" Jenna admonished.

"Don't worry, girl. You know I've got you covered. There is so much food you're tasting today, you won't have room for it all." Isabella hugged Becca's shoulders and moved to the first platter.

Becca appeared skeptical but remained silent.

"Now that you're all here, let's get started. This first set of samples are appetizers. These will be staged near the champagne fountain and vodka bar. Here you'll find six options. You can choose three from these. No substitutions or additions." Isabella made eye contact with each of us. "I mean it. No other suggestions. It's these or nothing."

The girl knew her audience, she gave us another hard glare just in case we hadn't caught her drift the first time. We had of course… caught ger drift the first time, so as a group we remained silent.

After each sample, we voted and then discussed the final selection.

But before we could move into the next course, Becca and Jenna got into an argument not really over which appetizer was better than the other but more about the way Becca announced her decision.

Becca's offending comment was, "The mushroom Wellington is way better than the shrimp wrap. We shouldn't have that at all. Who wants to walk around with shrimp breath?" And then Becca popped a shrimp wrap into her mouth… and moaned. Seriously, the sample she liked the least was still so good it was moan-worthy.

"Don't say that. That's rude to Isabella. All of the food is equally good." Sometimes it seemed Jenna's sole reason for walking the earth was to keep Becca in line. Not that it did any good. Becca did whatever she wanted… whenever she wanted. But it never slowed Jenna's determination to straighten out her friend.

Becca must have reached her monthly limit of being chastised. "I can' like the mushroom thingys more than the shrimp thingys if I want." She glared at Jenna and popped her last shrimp wrap sample into her mouth… and moaned again.

I looked at the others and quickly discovered by the look on her face that Terra was getting her feathers ruffled.

"Hey," I slapped my hand down on the marble island. "Let's not bicker during this. Okay?"

It would be easy for a comment to escalate and we'd lose one of them or even worse someone was going to get her feelings hurt and that's not how I wanted my wedding planning experience to be remembered.

"This is my wedding, and Isabella's food, so let's be sensitive about how we are speaking to and treating each other."

Jenna reached over and placed her hand on Becca's forearm. "I'll try to back off. My emotions are all tied up right now. I don't know what's going on with Marcus other than the guys have been working day in and day out and I miss him."

Becca hugged our friend. "I'll try to measure my words too, sis."

"Which one do you like?" I mumbled to Terra.

"I think anything Isabella makes is going to be delicious." Then she cleared her throat rather loudly and scanned the room until she had everyone's attention. "And since it's *your* wedding, Sydney, I think *your* vote should be the deciding factor."

"I think we'll do…" I started when Cabe and two of his partners Lucas and Marcus (the aforementioned Marcus who dated Jenna, but something was off and I hadn't had a chance to ask about it yet) entered the kitchen.

Well, it was more like they swaggered into the kitchen. The room suddenly filled with testosterone and charged energy. Cabe went directly to his wife and wrapped an arm around her waist to curl her into his side. Then his hand snaked out and he snatched up two of the prime rib and rosemary puff pastry appetizers.

"I told you not to come today." Isabella took his hands into hers and looked him in the eye. "What are you doing here? You're screwing up my vibe, babe."

"We thought it only right, our duty even, to stand in for our brother Roman since he can't be here." Lucas reached across Stella and helped himself to a handful of mushroom Wellingtons.

"Hey!" Becca yelled. "Not cool at all, man." She waved her hands over the island that held platters of the six appetizers prepared for my reception tasting. "These are ours. I haven't eaten in seventeen hours, waiting for this. Do not even think you are coming in here and gobbling them all up."

Lucas' dark gaze fixated on Becca. He tossed the stolen goods into his mouth and took a moment to savor the flavor before reaching past Stella once again and taking two more.

"That's enough!" Isabella said. "Take your men and leave here now or I won't make one single thing for you for an entire month."

Marcus, who had moved to stand behind Jenna during this exchange, leaned down and whispered in her ear, "Come with me."

I saw the Goosebumps rush across her skin.

"I'll see you girls later. Whatever you pick will be delicious." Jenna sent us air kisses. As they were leaving, I heard Marcus say, "I've got the next few hours free...."

I smiled to myself. Jenna deserved happiness. I wanted that for all of us but I wanted that for her most of all. I wanted her to know true love. I'm convinced she hasn't ever really known what it feels like to love that deeply.... or be loved that deeply.

I'm praying she finds it with Marcus.

"I call Jenna's portion!" Becca shouted over the arguing between Cabe and Isabella who was in the process of pushing her gorgeous husband out of the kitchen.

Lucas snatched a handful off of the platter, turned on his heel, and hightailed it out of the kitchen hot on Cabe's heels.

The energy in the room settled immediately and we let out a

collective sigh.

"Geez." Terra brought her wine glass to her lips for a sip.

"Lucas ate like six pieces. Whose portion is that coming from?" Becca glanced at Jenna's empty chair and relaxed.

"Don't worry. I made extra." Isabella was used to people gobbling up what she placed out so she'd begun reserving nearly half of what she had made. "We need to move along ladies or I'm going to run out of time."

Her assistant Stacy cleared away the empty appetizer platters. Isabella placed three large soup bowls on the island along with three warm cut-up loaves of bread. One had dried tomatoes on its crust and another had what looked like rosemary. Next, Stacy placed a handful of soup spoons and small tasting bowls on the counter. Isabella ladled the soup and we tried each one, dipping each type of bread, one by one to see which tasted best.

After a little discussion, we had a consensus. Also, I think Becca wasn't as hangry as she had been now that we were a couple of courses in.

"So everyone agrees, we are going with butternut squash soup with the rosemary focaccia bread." Isabella and Stacy cleared away the empty soup terrines and dishes. And brought out two salads.

Both were gorgeous and colorful. We ended up going with the cranberry walnut, blue cheese, and heirloom tomatoes.

Next up, the main course.

"I have a vegan choice as well. I think you had two people respond with a vegan request, anyway, it's a marinated and grilled cauliflower head with a spicy onion sauce over vegan risotto and sautéed vegetables." She looked around the island. "I didn't prepare any of that today. I hope it's okay."

"Thank God." Becca slouched in her chair. "I don't have much room left and we haven't even gotten to the main course yet."

20

No Matter

The mouth-watering delights Isabella and her team set before us, were serious show-stoppers. She had prime rib with garlic mashed potatoes and half a grilled artichoke that was so savory it fell apart at your fingertips. Next came a roasted quarter rosemary chicken, au gratin potatoes, and creamed spinach. And lastly, a chunky cioppino in a spicy red wine sauce with garlic toast points, and cheesy polenta.

"I feel like the cioppino, while delicious, might be messy to eat while everyone is dressed in formal attire and coats," Stella mumbled around her spoon.

"I agree, but can we put it on the menu for our New Year's Day brunch?" I sipped another spoonful savoring the spicy broth. "It would be delicious with Bloody Marys."

"And Champagne." Terra slurped her spoonful of goodness and winked at me. "Personally, I think you could just go with the prime rib and be done with it. Everyone loves a nice thick steak and the men will be especially thrilled."

"Oh, speaking of the men, before I forget, Francesca found a sweet vintage wagon and she stripped that baby down, then added electricity, a sink, and a small ice maker for a whiskey and cigar bar. Between that and the steak Roman will want to get married every year."

The funny part is, when I made that statement, I believed it. But at that time, I had no idea what would be in store for us and you know sometimes things don't always go as we hoped.

"A vodka bar *and* a whiskey bar?" Becca's mouth hung open.

"Nothing crazy, maybe five or so top-shelf whiskeys and a handful of cigars."

"This is going to be the best wedding ever!" Becca twirled around and danced a little jig.

"I think she might be more excited than you are." Terra sipped her champagne and winked at me.

"Since we aren't having seafood for an appetizer or main course, would you be open to a shrimp cocktail course at the start of the meal?" Isabella was a master hostess and hospitality was her gift. She had a gift to know exactly what to do to level up any event she was involved in. You could count on her contribution to be of utmost excellence.

"If you're willing to make them, I'm willing to pay for them." I didn't care how much this cost. It was the price Roman was going to pay for this crazy deadline and not helping me with the planning. Even if I did think he was going to have the time of his life.

"I'm going to have to fast until your wedding," Becca mumbled.

"You're the smallest of all of us, why would you need to fast?" Isabella asked.

"Pft." Becca waved her hand. "Has nothing to do with my waistline and everything to do with making sure I have enough room for all of this delicious food. I'm not the only one who will hurt herself... or himself to finish one of your meals." She pointed her finger at Isabella. "They won't know that the food is going to keep on coming." Becca shook her head. "I'm telling you, people are going to hurt themselves."

"I've got some black pastry boxes we can set out for people who want to take food home if you like?"

"I like that idea. I won't have to worry about what to do with the leftovers and you won't have to worry about bringing it home."

"Honestly, it's like a wedding favor," Becca snickered.

"Actually, that's a great idea," Terra said. "Let's set a table up with pastry boxes, take away utensils, to-go bags, the works. We will put signs up and let everybody know to make sure that they are to take food home." She looked at Isabella and then me, "do you think it would be all right if Isabella made extra large portions?"

I shrugged my shoulders. "Because it's Christmas Eve it's going to be a small party. It's fine to pay a little bit extra to make sure everyone who gives their Christmas Eve to us has more than enough to eat."

"*Jumping Jezebels* Cabe is going to lose his mind! You know he is going to try to take as much of the leftovers as he can?" Isabella laughed. "He'll see it as a challenge."

We laughed because Cabe was exactly like that. Even at Francesca's husband's funeral, Cabe was monitoring how much everyone, especially the men, ate and would try to stop people from filling their plates. Most of us have learned to ignore him. Luckily, his hands will be full with the twins who want to be everywhere. Fathers of daughters are a special breed, and he was one of the best.

"I think this sounds wonderful and it will all be a surprise to Roman." I laughed at my best friends. "I think my only competition will be the food! I'll tell you right now... if he spends more time thinking about Isabella's food than his bride who jumped through flaming hoops of fire, he won't make it through to his honeymoon!" I may or may not have stomped my foot. I definitely slapped my hand down in the cool marble and my sisters cheered and clapped.

We toasted and emptied our glasses.

"I have an idea about the wedding cake." Isabella was ready to move on. "I think we have a normal-sized cake at the bridal table for the bridal party. But, we have three tiered replicates as centerpieces with red roses cascading down the side and along the bottom. We can wrap miniature battery-operated lights throughout the roses. It would be stunning and with the take-home box idea, this would be a great addition. Every table gets their own cake and whatever is left over they get to take home." She stopped talking and noticed that our mouths were hanging open.

Terra was the first one to recover. "Are you sure you can handle all of that? That's a lot of cakes."

"Stacy and I went over it. The icing will be plain white cream with a few adornments, the biggest pop on the cakes will be the red roses and Stacy can do those no problem."

"Yippee!" Becca whooped it up. "This is going to be the best dang wedding ever! All the bitches around here are going to want one just like this!"

"Only if they can pay for it," Isabella mumbled.

"Here here." Terra smiled at Isabella. "I think with some crystal candelabras and flickering candlelight the table cakes are a great idea. I love it." Terra looked to the sisters, Jules and Stella. "How are the boa wreaths coming along?"

The sisters rolled their eyes. Stella was the only one to speak, "Well…. There's something we need to share about the wreaths…."

21

What Life

"If I never see another feather boa as long as I live it'll be too soon." Stella was attaching the handmade white feather boa wreaths to the backs of the chairs complaining the entire time. Jules had just about enough of her sister's moaning and groaning. I could see the steam starting to puff from her red ears. Turns out the only issue with the boa wreaths were the sisters put in charge of making them. I wasn't sure what was going on with the two of them but they had been going at it like teenagers for a few days now. Every meeting and anytime we were together they'd separate like they couldn't stand to be in the same room with one another.

"Why don't I help?" I asked to help alleviate some of the burdens. It was the least I could do. The wedding was almost here. Just one more night and I'd be waking up to the happiest day of my life. The small feather wreaths were gorgeous. We were attaching them with a thick red velvet ribbon and Jules was following behind and adding a decorative bow made from the same ribbon. Simple but festive.

I looked around at the 4 F Ranch and couldn't believe the transformation that had taken place. A blanket of soft whites and cream in various textures covering the entire ranch. Francesca was at that very moment accepting the fourth and final delivery of white poinsettias that she was stacking one right next to another. It created a rolling hill of white, gold, and cream.

Terra and Jenna were working on the Christmas Trees. The walkways and along the aisle to the gazebo which would become our altar for the service were bordered by sparkling white lights and flocked trees wrapped in white flickering lights, of all shapes and sizes.

I took my phone out to check to see if Roman had texted me back. Still nothing. Now I was beginning to get worried. I swore to him I wouldn't micromanage his time when he was on a big case but this was ridiculous. He had been on much bigger cases than the one he was currently working but he'd always check in with me. I decided since my phone was out I'd capture all of the wedding planning to share with my groom once he decided to show his gorgeous self.

I snapped photos moving throughout the decorating and deliveries. I ended up a few feet from Francesca when the last poinsettias were finally offloaded and she placed them in the last bare spot.

My breath caught. She'd pulled off giving me the white Christmas I'd asked for. I spun around and took it all in. Over near the fire pits, Becca was fighting with a ladder. Sophie and Fallon were helping to string the miles of crystal-encrusted pearl garlands over the guest tables.

A million white lights were strung overhead. Flocked trees covered with white lights were everywhere. As soon as the sun lowered from the sky this was going to be brilliant.

The whiskey and cigar bar was set up with wine barrel-style tables with stools crowded around. Crystal ashtrays were being set out, along with crystal tumblers that had S&R and our wedding date engraved into them.

I snatched one up. "Who had time to do this?"

Stella pointed to where Francesca was busy helping her ranch hands place the last few flocked trees that had been delivered. She hadn't heard me shout. I counted the tumblers and noted that she had fifty. "Are these favors too?"

My friend smiled at me. I spun around taking everything in. They'd done this for me.

"I'll be right back." I handed over the ribbon I'd been working with to tie the wreath to the chair.

I walked briskly but, in all honesty, it took every bit of self-control to stop myself from running to where the champagne fountain was currently being set up. They were already stacking the champagne saucers on top of each other forming a pyramid so it was easy to slip one out and inspect it.

"Hunh." I set the saucer down and smiled at the person who was busy unwrapping them. Nothing had been engraved on these.

I headed to the vodka bar and noticed they were setting out the clear shot glasses. I snatched one as it was unwrapped and there it was! The same S&R with the date of our wedding as the whiskey tumblers. I felt a little letdown but not because the whiskey and vodka bars got the special glassware, but because I hadn't thought of it sooner myself and made it happen. Leaving the shot glasses, I made my way toward the house where I passed two Bellini Estate staff hauling two large containers on wheels to where the wedding preparations were happening. Something had me swiveling and following the pair as they painstakingly transported their burden to its destination. I knew in my soul these were what I was looking for. I knew Isabella had done the thing her aunt would have. Before I knew what hit me, all these memories of Raquel's wedding washed over me and I stumbled.

Becca must have been watching because the next thing I heard was, "Girl you best not be getting ready to hurt yourself before you have to walk your butt down the aisle."

I laughed, stumbled again, and started crying. I put my hands to my face overwhelmed with emotions and sank to my rear. I let all the emotions I'd been holding back, rush over me. Friends, and the only real family I'd ever known, weren't going to be here to see me join myself to the only man who has ever mattered to me.

It wasn't fair.

It wasn't fucking fair that she wasn't there to yell at me for taking this precious time to feel sorry for myself. It wasn't fucking fair that Antonio wasn't here to give Roman a hard time, to make him promise to care for me under threat of death and dismemberment, like all big brothers would, blood or not. Family is exactly what these people had been to me.

It was too much. It was all too much and I was overwhelmed. Before I could muster myself, I felt arms embracing me and someone stroking my hair but I didn't have the strength to pull my head out of my hands and see who it was.

"What happened?" That was Francesca, out of breath from running over as soon as she saw one of her sisters go down.

"She collapsed when I yelled at her." Becca was the strong arms surrounding me. She was tiny in stature but between her personality and her heart she was the biggest of all of us... and I'd always have her.

"Babe, what's going on with you?" Francesca whispered.

I was sitting on the ground surrounded by the women who loved me most in the world, being held up by them.

"Raquel should be here with us. No matter what it takes or how hard I have to fight I vow to make those fucking bastards pay for what their son did to Raquel and Antonio!"

"Well, I did bash his head in." Isabella hadn't had a choice about bashing his head in, but he'd left her no choice. He was going to feed her and her mother to pigs and take the winery for his family.

I looked up, surprised that Isabella was so close. I soon realized every single one of the girls who'd seen me drop had dropped what they were doing and had their arms wrapped around me.

"I know you did honey." She carried that demon around with her and often the nightmare that was her real life had her sitting straight up in the middle of the night drenched in sweat. I knew it because it happened to me and Sophie too.

"It doesn't seem like enough. We all have to suffer the loss. They stole them from us. I want her here to see me marry the man of my dreams." I shook my head. "For so long I thought if I ever got married Antonio would walk me down the aisle..."

"Why don't you save all your pent-up rage and seek vengeance on the fucker who is still bugging our houses? I mean, he could get one of us offed at any time, like he almost did Jenna." Becca had a good point. I stopped crying.

"Yeah." I wiped my tears. "I could do that."

"Don't let Cabe hear you say that." Isabella looked over her shoulder.

"Laird either, he would lose his shit if he thought for one moment we were putting ourselves in harm's way again." Francesca gave me big eyes.

"When has what the men ... or any man... thought ever been a deciding factor for our tribe?" Becca put her hands on her hips. "We'll circle back around to that topic later, but for right now, we can't do anything to keep Raquel and Antonio alive." Becca had lowered her voice. "But we can do stuff to keep us bitches alive now. That's what we should focus on. Save talk about Raquel for midnight margarita discussions... if you know what I mean."

I didn't totally know what she meant however, you know you really needed to take a step back and look at your thought processes when Becca seemed to be the reasonable one.

"So, with that said, I'm in on operation vengeance, or operation keep the bitches alive, whichever. But do you think we can get your butt married first?" Becca hadn't pulled any punches but she had also stroked my hair through her tough love speech.

We agreed it best to stick with the task at hand, go after the hacker who we decided needed a nickname, and then after the first of the year move to operation vengeance. I liked this anyway because it gave me a chance to stew on all the angles we could come at him.

Later that night...

Francesca was exhausted from the weeks of long hours she'd been putting in. It was a labor of love and therefore even though she was past tired she felt good. Things were moving ahead. Laird had come around and the two of them were moving forward in a way where she could see a future with the big Scots.

Of course, as things will be, no sooner had she thought that than the big lug pulled his large shiny truck into the barn and started unloading something.

She couldn't make out what he was moving from the bed of his truck, but she knew one thing for sure. He was not going to mess up her barn. She'd finally gotten it dialed in perfectly. One thing out of place and it would disrupt her system. Okay, maybe she was being a tiny bit dramatic but dammit, this was her barn and she wanted it how she wanted it.

She switched direction and with a deep sigh headed back toward the large barn that she had recently built to replace the one that had been lost to the last wildfire. The same fire that was her husband's demise. Now to be fair, the man was on his last leg, but the fire raged through the community and was the ultimate cause of the dying man's death. Ironic, isn't it?

Life could be weird sometimes.

As she drew closer to the barn, she could hear Laird's music coming from the cab of his truck and she smiled to herself. He loved American classic rock. His current selection was Lynyrd Skynyrd's Gimme Three Steps. It was impossible not to bounce to the beat as she entered the barn. Laird was closing the back stall and caught her as she entered.

"Hey, there handsome. Whatcha doing out here? You're not messing up my barn, are you?"

The look that washed over Laird's face made Francesca stop in her tracks. She'd just caught him. Doing what? She had no idea. But, he was up to something, she knew it.

"Whatever you are up to, now is not the time."

That made Laird halt his approach.

"What do ye mean lass?"

"What I mean is exactly what I said. Sydney's wedding can't have any problems and you are the officiant, be cool."

Laird laughed. "Be cool ye say?" And continued his approach.

Francesca squinted at him. He was definitely up to something. She took a step back instinctively. Laird's step faltered. Francesca had to be careful. This is the way great sex happened with the man.

"I don't have time to be chased down and ravaged." Francesca didn't mean to smile while she said it. It came out of her mouth against her will. Her face and voice acting of their own volition. One thing she did know was that it definitely did the opposite of her intention. Instead of slowing down or stopping his approach, he smiled at her and picked up his pace. Which did nothing more than make her step back, again.

"Ye know if ye run what will happen." Laird's mood shifted. It was dark and predatory. Francesca felt him to her core and something primal struck. She didn't know what kind of magic the big Scots had or why he had such a pull over her... but damn if he didn't awaken every feminine instinct in her to claim her man.

She watched his dark head as he moved closer to her. He was so beautiful; it was almost too hard to believe he was hers.

But was he? Was he really? Fear of loss was running rampant and soon her thoughts turned to all that she'd lost in the last year. The loss that began way before ... years before.

She shook her head and looked at her feet.

"What happened, lass?" She looked up to see Laird standing directly in front of her. The look on his face matched the concerned tone in his voice.

"Sometimes things shift on me and I need a minute to adjust, is all." Suddenly she felt shy and before she knew what was happening... a tear rolled down her face.

"Oh lass, what has ye fretting?"

"Nothing." Without her permission, a second tear rolled.

Laird gripped her upper arms gently and pulled the beautiful woman to him. This was going to be the hardest 24 hours of his life. He'd already procured the only permission he needed to make this gorgeous woman his... he just had to be patient. But her standing before him with tears filling her eyes wasn't helping his resolve to stick to the plan.

"I'm a daydreamer whose world has crashed to the ground around her. I'd been living with my head in the clouds not preparing well enough for the future and it was time reality became my first priority."

Laid wasn't sure he liked the way that sounded. He had already made plans for their future and cleared it with her two daughters. They were already a team. She just didn't know it yet.

For the first time in his life, he was unsure how to proceed. Did he say fuck it and propose to her right here and now in the barn? Or did he try to ride it out and stick to the plan that he and the girls had set forth?

The thought of disappointing his future daughters didn't suit him. He would not begin his lifelong relationship with them by going against their well-thought-out plan. It would be a form of betrayal. He took in his beauty and gently pressed her head to his chest. As she settled in, he wrapped his arms around her and rested his chin on top of her head.

This was everything he'd been missing in his life.

Exactly what he'd been craving and needed more than he needed his right arm or leg. Emotion caught in his chest. He was finally going to have a family of his own. Finally belonging to something good and right. It was almost too good to be true that he was not only getting this gorgeous wild woman in his arms but he got the honor of helping her to raise her daughters too. Nothing was more precious than trusting him to share in the responsibility... and the treasure of her family. He sure the fuck wasn't going to do anything to fuck it up before it got started.

Just as he had that last thought, Faith cleared her throat from the barn door. "If you two think you can pry yourselves apart there was a delivery."

Francesca lifted her head but didn't release her hold on Laird. "What else could it be? The trees and poinsettias were delivered."

Faith held up a smallish box and rattled it. "I doubt there's a flocked tree in this."

"Oh! I know what it is!" And just like that, her mood shifted from sad to excited. Laird was never going to be used to the vast range of emotions he experienced with his girls... his girls.

His girls.

Damn, he thought. That felt good. It took everything in his power not to drop to his knee and declare his undivided love and devotion to her and her beautiful daughters. Beg her to make him the luckiest man in the world. For sure luckier than he deserved.

Francesca ripped away from his arms and ran to her daughter.

"It's the rings!" She screamed. Faith screamed and jumped up and down before high tailing it out of the barn completely forgetting Laird and what she'd almost caught him doing.

22

Brings Us

The private jet landed smoothly. Lydia Ivanov played with the 4-carat black solitaire hanging off a platinum chain from around her neck. The stone had been gifted to her by the only man she'd ever deemed worthy of her... until he was lost like everything decent in life. It was snuffed out. Only the hardest survived. She crossed her ankles and rested against the back of the luxurious leather seat until her two enforcers gave the all-clear to disembark.

The staccato from her six-inch stiletto metal heels reverberated off of the private airport hangar walls. The limo door popped open as she approached and she transitioned inside flawlessly.

Sure she was a well-respected assassin in her own right... owned a small slice of the criminal activity in Russia, but she wasn't here in that capacity.

Lydia loved nothing more than being true to who she was in the moment. At this particular time, she was a *Bratva* Princess ready to embark on her Queendom. If only the self-righteous jerk that her family had ridiculously betrothed her to when she was far too young to know what that even meant... would fall in line like she herself had all these years.

She couldn't be the only one who felt family and honor were above all else. Could she? It was impossible to know how this would go. Americans were so self-righteous and entitled to their imagined freedoms. She knew better. Everyone had to fall in line.

Everyone.

It was up to each person to decide what that line looked like. Lydia for instance decided she really wasn't interested in being a passive pawn among powerful men. Instead, she embraced her role as the *Bratva* princess that she was and molded the role to look how she wanted, instead of how others told her it was supposed to be.

Another lesson she learned very early on, it was better to apologize than to ask for permission. Lydia never asked if she could do something, she just did it. For instance, being a princess of the Russian Lord she was taught how to be a perfect lady. Perfect and proper in all things. But, when she wanted to learn how to use knives & blades, she didn't even bother to ask her parents. One, her mother would absolutely forbid it. Two, her father would be outraged that she dared to take on anything that was meant for men. Her father had very clear lines about what was proper for men and what was proper for young ladies. And the two should not cross.

So, she found her own weapons expert and learned each discipline one by one on her own with none the wiser. She learned about explosives from a terrorist group in Afghanistan. From Israel, she learned handguns, sniping, and hand-to-hand combat. She learned the art of poison, not only how to administer it but how to grow and make it, from a 97-year-old man in Taiwan. She learned how to clean a crime scene in London, and how to hack government agency websites and databases in the US. She learned how to create documents... or get rid of troublesome information, from a brilliant Italian.

Her parents believed her to be on shopping trips.

She networked herself. She took small jobs and worked her way up.

She built her own underground reputation separate from her public persona as her father's Russian mafia princess.

By the time her father discovered her dual identity, it was too late. She was too powerful for even him. The old man would attempt to bully her on the holidays, and during many family get-togethers. But she held fast.

Her mother was something else entirely.

Her father could never bring himself to cross the line from personal to business. He left her alone, and she continued to grow.

She watched the landscape entranced by rows upon rows of vineyards.

"There are so many beautiful vineyards."

"*Da.*" Her eyes flit to the driver when he replied. He wasn't hers.

"*Sebastian?*" Lydia asked in Russian.

"*Da.*" His dark eyes followed her in the rearview mirror.

"You gorgeous son of a bitch. How have you been?" Lydia's eyes sparkled with mischief.

"Not as good as you, it seems."

"Me?"

"*Da.* I have my little sliver of happiness while you are next in line for the throne."

Lydia had heard this before.

"Pfftt." She waved her perfectly manicured hand. "A throne I want no part of. I don't need that old dusty thing. I'm building a bright shiny new one of my very own." She touched the black diamond on her chest. "Let it die with the old men," she said softly.

"You know better. Too much power in one place. Someone else will step up if you do not. When the old pass, the young are eager and ever-waiting, ready to snatch what they believe to be their right. They won't be nice about it. When your old man passes you make sure you're protected. *Da?*"

125

Lydia watched the back of Sebastian's head intently.

"They will come for you, Lydia, before your *oteu's* body is cold. Some will decide you are the key to the kingdom and try to rope you into a deal through a marriage union. Others won't be so nice about it, they may decide force is fine, or even remove you entirely. You need to get your head about you. You need to beef up your security and get smart."

"*Da,*" she agreed, nodding her head even though he couldn't see her. She waved her hand. "I will simply renounce my rights to the old Bratva." Lydia watched as row upon row of grape vines passed by the window.

Sebastian shook his head. "You're too big of a threat. You'd undermine their authority in their eyes. They won't want the competition your father tolerated. They also won't allow you to keep the wealth you've generated. Someone will want it for themselves. They will see it as booty deserved to them simply because they can take it from you."

Lydia sat back. She'd never considered that the reason the *Bratva* had never come for her was because of her father's interference.

"Shit," she whispered. The few times there were crossovers between her business and the *Bratva*, they always withdrew. Every single time.

How dumb could she be? Her father had been manipulating her all along.

"…. a young man will want your piece too." Sebastian had been talking but she'd missed most of it. "Your father kept the others from coming for you. He protected you and your portion of the pie. Now you will be fair game."

"If everything you say is true, then I guess I'll be inheriting a dusty old throne after all." This didn't make her happy. Nor did it fit well into the plans she had for herself.

"*Da.* Check it out for yourself. I have nothing to gain from telling you this except to see you next year and the year after, happy and content."

She leaned forward and patted her old friend's shoulder. "Thank you, dear friend. You have saved my future self from much turmoil..." she sat back and mumbled, "and possibly my life."

"I hate to continue to be the bearer of bad news, but you may want to consider making an alliance with a strong male who can protect you."

"What do you mean, Sebastian? This is why I am here. To collect my groom."

"No. You won't get Romanov. He is lost to you. Look elsewhere."

"I will not." It was a matter of pride. She just needed time to think about this new news. Romanov was the perfect solution and besides, he was her right. He had to know her father would not look kindly on his refusing her.

Time to have a candid discussion with the old man.

And Sebastian wasn't wrong. She would need to align herself with someone strong. Maybe a financial arrangement. That way the cards were face up on the table and it wouldn't go sideways.

She had been so naive to think the *Bratva* had left her alone to amass a fortunate and small army because they feared her. She had been fooling herself. They'd see it as a challenge. No self-respecting Russian *Bratva* enforcer would be able to do anything less than fight to the death; for honor if nothing else.

This meant she needed Romanov now more than ever.

"He will be mine. He has to be." Lydia played with her black diamond. "Aleks will see it my way. He is a reasonable man who understands the importance of the old traditions."

"Roman's uncle will not force him to marry you."

"We shall see now, shan't we?"

"Do not do this thing, Lydia. It won't go for you the way you hope."

She leaned forward. "Do you approve of Romanov's little American, Sebastian?"

"*Da.* She has the heart of a Russian. She is a fighter. And a good match for Roman."

"Roman."

"Da. He is American. He isn't *Romanov*, and he isn't going to abandon his life to run away with you to Russia and become your arm candy."

Lydia leaned back and flicked her wrist. "Maybe I need to arrange a meet-up with his little distraction myself."

Sebastian's hard eyes focused on her in the rear view mirror.

23

We Are Forever

The weeks leading up to my wedding... I mean ... *our* wedding... flew by at lightning speed.

Seriously. It wasn't hard to keep the girls distracted. We did literally everything ourselves. We were in the middle of stringing the pearl garlands that were to be wrapped around the white lights, and then wrapped around the flocked trees and draped along the aisle.

We were at Terra's sprawling California Bungalow sitting in front of her roaring person-sized fireplace ...which was total overkill in my opinion, but whatever, nobody asked me. There was a tree on either side of the huge fire decorated with deep blue velvet ribbon and large gold ornaments. Terra's style has always been "big". Her heels were big, her hair was big, and her house was big. She was the only tiny thing in her oversized world. Her place was decorated to the nines. The Christmas decorations were elegant and classy despite being oversized. Her color scheme this year was royal blue and gold. The mantel over her humongous fireplace was buried under a heavily decorated garland.

It was stunning.

Stella, Jules, Francesca, and her youngest daughter Faith, along with

Jenna were busy stringing endless strands of twenty-foot pearl garland. Terra and I were bringing the next batch of margaritas out from the kitchen because this shit was boring, we needed something to liven the place up.

I was bored and it was my wedding.

In an attempt to liven up the mood, I synced one of my party playlists with Terra's epic surround sound with Boom Boom by the Animals and a party was born.

I had a playlist for everything. Need to fall asleep? I've got soothing tunes that will knock you on your butt. Want to work out? I have exactly what the trainer ordered. Romance? Yeah, I have four playlists dedicated to the art of romance and which vibe I'm aiming at. For instance, If I want it hot and dirty I'd play Brick House or Mr. Bone. If I wanted it slow and sexy I'd play the playlist with songs like All of Me.

I love my playlists. They were part of my routine and I considered them a valuable tool for my mental and emotional health, which also meant the rest of the world was safe.

Me being a first-rate bridezilla, I'd had the girls running from the time they rose until they collapsed exhausted into their beds each night. I felt bad for working them to death but their efforts were spectacular. The black satin bridesmaids' dresses were finished, along with their fitted capes. The simple rose bouquets will look great against the black.

We sang along with the music, most of us off-key, danced a bit and finished every last bit of wedding duties.

Note to self, anytime things are dragging add alcohol and music. We enjoyed each other until the sun began to set in the sky.

"Well ladies, I believe it's time for me to return home to spend my last evening as a single woman." It was finally time to head home and settle in for the evening.

"Where are you staying tonight?" Becca asked.

"At home."

"You're not supposed to be home! You're supposed to be with your maid of honor."

"And my maid of honor lives with me... at my home... where I'll be."

"Oh." Becca didn't seem settled with this answer. "Where will Roman stay?"

"I have no idea." I looked around. "I have to be honest, girls. I haven't spoken or heard from Roman in a couple of days. He warned me this might happen so I'm trying not to freak out ... but, I'm starting to freak out."

The room was still, no one moved.

"Anyone else feel chills run over their skin?" Becca shivered.

"Are you serious?" Terra asked me.

"I'm serious." I shook my head. "But he did warn me this might happen."

"What did he say?"

"He said what he always says when he is working on a really big case. That I might not hear from him. And then he said that he had to deal with something I'd been *trying*," my eyes landed on Becca, "to keep from your focus but now I guess I don't need to worry about it since the wedding is tomorrow."

I took a deep breath. "Roman was betrothed."

"A what?" Jules' face scrunched.

"He was promised at birth to a Russian woman who has decided to come claim her man!" Becca said excitedly.

I stared open-mouthed at her.

"What? I can keep a secret. Bet you thought all this time I couldn't keep my mouth shut. You didn't, did ya?"

"You never stop amazing me." I smiled. She hadn't exactly kept my secret... but that she tried said a lot about her and how she felt about me. It's what people show you after all - not what they tell you, that matters.

"Thank you." I surprised us both by popping up and bear-hugging her from behind. We both laughed when I tried to lift her and couldn't. "*Lord Almighty,* you're heavy for a little thing!" I swiped the tears from my cheeks. My jaw hurt from laughing so hard.

Becca held her skinny arm up in the strong man pose and slapped her bicep.

"It's all muscle baby!"

I laid my head on her shoulder. "I love you."

She patted my head. "Back at ya, babe."

"Can we talk about this Russian who is coming for Roman?" Terra was standing with her hands on her slender hips.

"Tomorrow is the wedding. I don't think it's a problem."

"But do you know? Maybe this is why you haven't heard from Roman."

"He said he was going to handle it."

"Why don't you call the station and be sure he is at least showing up for work."

A sick feeling washed over me. I was smarter than this. I knew better. I should have checked in on him by now. The wedding planning was making me crazy.

"I swear on all that is holy if she got her claws into him and he has been with her all this time he is going to get it good!"

"What if she is holding him hostage and he can't get away?" Terra was watching me closely. I honestly couldn't tell you what I was feeling at that moment except for complete rage.

"This is Roman Stognafsky we are talking about. If he wanted to escape, he would!" I shouted because I needed to yell. "You guys are freaking me out! What if she does have him? Or what if one of the seven thousand other bad guys that he has arrested has him? And I waited all this time to alert someone?"

"Now listen babe, I think we're gonna be fine, let's not get ahead of ourselves, maybe we should call the station now and leave a message for him to call you back." Terra was already in management mode. I could see the worry and concern written all over her face. Becca had moved to stand beside me and put her arm around my waist. Their comfort helped but also made it apparent that they thought something was wrong too.

The facts were, shit happened to us. Our friends had been murdered, I've been kidnapped, Sophie had been kidnapped and brutalized. I'd almost been killed by the Russian mafia before that. Isabella had been terrorized, not to mention Jenna. And we still couldn't find the guy responsible for bugging her entire house and selling it to the highest bidder online.

He was still out there. We had every right to be upset and concerned. And I was just big enough of a jerk not to have thought about all this. About how this was so out of character for Roman that it didn't make any sense at all that he wouldn't have at least texted me back.

I needed to do something and I needed to do it right away.

First off, I texted Roman again. Then called him and left a message when he didn't reply. Next thing we did was call the station and left a message for his partner and his boss to call. I had left so many messages on his desk phone and so far, he had not returned one of them so I didn't think I needed to do that again.

We called back and asked if someone could check to see if Roman Stognafsky had been to work the last two days. The officer who took my call had no idea who I was and was less than forthcoming with information. Nor did he give the impression that he was going to explore my concerns further. I knew from experience, once a cop shut you down that was it. I found them for the most part to be very rigid in their flexibility or lack thereof.

There was nothing left for me to do but wait for Roman's partner or boss to get my messages. Until then I was doing the next best thing. I called Cabe and sicced him on Roman's trail. At first, he was reluctant but when I told him I hadn't heard from him in more than 24 hours he said he would look into it. I must admit, it helped knowing he was on the job. Worst-case scenario, Roman is pissed that I made such a big deal out of him not checking in and learns he needs to make contact once within a 24-hour period. Either way, I felt much better once I hung up with Cabe.

With that done I decided I wanted to go home and wait for him there. I felt a strong need to be in my own space and I thought maybe he might've gone home. I needed to check to see if his clothes had been changed or if there were any signs at all that he had been home. I could check the security and see if he had been there.

We made short work of cleaning up, got everything ready for the next day which would be my wedding day, and one by one we left Terra's home. I made it out to the Range Rover and onto the road. I pulled up to my house and noticed that there was a long black sedan parked in a manner that blocked my front door. I pulled around back like I normally would, and went in through the glass doors near my office. Before I could shut the door and disarm the alarm I was shoved inside.

"Not this again, goddamnit!"

This was the second time that somebody had come into my home, this very home, the third time overall. I was getting damn sick and tired of having the place that I lived in, a place that I was supposed to be able to be at my most vulnerable broken in to. After all, it's what drove me from my country and my friends almost seven years ago.

"You must be Sydney." I heard a thick Russian accent. Definitely female. I turned and found the source and came face-to-face with a tall blonde brick house that was stunning from head to toe. She was dressed in a black fitted double-breasted Prada suit with patent leather stiletto pumps. Her white blonde hair was slicked back and fell about her shoulders in a controlled curl. A large black diamond pendant sparkled at the base of her neck. She was taller than me, wider than me, curvier than me, and by my standards much prettier than me. My stomach dropped, had Roman seen her? If he had, had he been as enamored as I was?

"My name is Sydney," I said with a shaky voice. "Roman isn't here, but I bet you know that already, don't you?"

"*Da.* I've been looking everywhere for *Romanov.* So far, he has eluded me. But, I figured if I had you he would eventually come to me."

I didn't like the way that sounded. The last thing I wanted was to spend the night before my wedding with the woman who came to claim my husband-to-be. Even though I knew she probably wouldn't care that I was supposed to get married the next day, I had to at least see if she had an ounce of understanding and kindness in her.

"Listen, tomorrow is supposed to be the happiest day of my life. I am getting married to the man that I have been in love with for seven years. A man I never thought I was good enough to have. But he showed me that he couldn't live without me. Me!" I pointed at my chest. "Now, the last thing I'm gonna let happen is you get in the way of that. If you think about it, I saved his life. So, he would've died if it hadn't been for me so he owes me." I shrugged my shoulders. "Besides, I love him."

She watched me with her ice-blue eyes. "*Da.* There is some truth to that, I can see your thought process." She reached up and jerked the chain from around her neck until she held the beautiful black diamond up to the light. "I hold before you one of my most prized possessions. It's worth $2.4 million. I will happily hand it over to you for *Romanov.*"

This bitch wasn't getting it. There was no way I was trading that handsome hunk of mine for a freaking diamond. She had no idea who I was, or who Roman was. If she did, she would never have offered something so paltry. He was priceless. And that's what I told her.

"There's absolutely nothing on this earth you could trade me for. If you had any idea who Roman was you would never have offered. I will never give up on him."

"I was afraid of that. It would've been nice if you had taken the diamond. I hate having to destroy beautiful creatures such as yourself. But, things must be done. I'm afraid I can't afford not to take *Romanov* back with me."

"If you kill me, he will never go with you. He will seek revenge. You'll have to kill him too."

"*Da*, I agree. That's why it would've been so much easier if you had just accepted the diamond. But, as long as I have you, I have something to leverage. And leverage you, I shall." She flipped her head at her henchmen and he stepped towards me.

I stepped back, and put my hands up, but there was nothing I could do. The large man put his shoulder to my belly and up I went over his back. I'd been carried this way so many times in the last year that it was becoming redundant. Or, even worse, I was getting used to it - I wasn't sure which. They took me to the waiting sedan. The Russian princess slid in and her henchman shoved me in after.

By the time I sat up I was fit to be tied.

"You realize tomorrow is my wedding day? Right?" I looked around frantically, I'd left my phone in my purse and it was in my house.

"*Da*. Sebastian may have mentioned it." She flipped her hand as if to wave away the importance of the event.

"Sebastian? You can't tell me that he helped you. I know that would be a lie, he would never betray me in this way. He would never betray Aleks, and he would certainly never betray Roman!"

"Right again. You'll be happy to know, he warned me off of you. Which only served to make me more curious." She looked me up and down and I wondered what she saw. I looked down at myself, I'd just come from a full day of wedding decorating following the previous evening of drinking, dancing, and singing with my sisters. I'm sure

I didn't look my best, it made me sit up a little bit and suck in my tummy... not that I had a big stomach, I didn't... but I still sucked it in.

"I can see your charm. I'm not surprised Roman would desire to have a quality woman such as yourself at his side." The car's motor hummed and we pulled out of the driveway. My blood pressure skyrocketed. I knew as soon as we drove out of my driveway, chances were good I may not be seen again. "But if he thinks you are a strong partner to him, surely he would see me as an even stronger partner."

"See, that's where you don't know Roman at all. It isn't about strength or leveraging our relationship. It's about being in love and depending on each other."

Lydia let out a sharp laugh. "Don't kid yourself, every relationship is transactional in one way or another."

"Well then, if you're going to put it that way I still win! I've saved his life. I'm not sure how you're going to be able to equal that transaction."

Screw this bitch if she thought she was going to talk me down from marrying the man of my dreams. She had no idea who she was messing with. I may not have a fancy Russian title and I may not have killed anybody... at least on purpose.... But, nobody, and I mean nobody, was going to stop me from becoming Mrs. Roman Stognafsky. I didn't care how old-fashioned that sounded. I was no traditional woman. I'd lived an independent international lifestyle for many years. I didn't need anyone to take care of me, because I could do that just fine on my own.

But snuggling with that giant man of mine? His sexy growl? His spicy musk smell? Our midnight swims? Nothing compared to that. Those were the moments I lived for. You know what's even better? Those were the moments Roman lived for too. He made sure I knew it, every single day.

Each one we could eek out was our reward for doing the right thing and managing to remain alive. He was my reward and I was his.

We worked to do what we thought was right. And let me tell you, it was hard damn work. Long days and late nights. But if it's important, it's worth working for. Roman has his job, one that is arguably one of the most important. I have Safe Haven. A home I established to help girls and women who had been victimized by human trafficking. We both dealt with heavy stuff on a day-to-day basis. This is why I knew Roman would never ever, even as big of a jerk as he had been, ever abandon me for this tall ice queen, no matter how powerful or beautiful she was.

Period. End of story.

I was beginning to feel a little more confident. "Roman isn't going to marry you." I leaned toward her and lowered my voice. "I want to be sure you understand what I am saying, it's not that he isn't going to marry *you*. You're beautiful. I'm sure you're very rich, you'd be anyone's dream wife." It was true. She was stunning in a cold aloof sort of way. Her curvy body and long ice-blond hair were only enhanced by her dark eyebrows.

My eyes landed on the large black diamond pendant twinkling at her neck.

"Nothing will keep Roman from marrying *me*." I leaned back and looked her up and down again, making sure she saw my eyes. I hoped she felt them on her. *"This is beneath you. Why are you prostrating like this?"* I said in Russian. I'd been working on my new second language as a Christmas present for Roman that would now transfer to also being a wedding present … and I was now hoping it would lend to saving my life.

She leaned back and looked me in the eye, apparently judging my honesty. Her head twitched and she looked out the window.

"I can't leave without a strong man at my side. My world isn't as fair or safe as yours." Her words were spoken softly, her Russian perfect.

Seriously? She came all this way just to marry anyone?

"You've been stressing my groom out and him being stressed ruined our wedding ring shopping." I watched her deflate. Her heart wasn't into this kidnapping. I felt less in danger and a little more curious. "What's going on, sister?"

Her eyes flew to mine before she dug around in her bag. "I just learned that all the power and wealth I thought I'd obtained was only due to the protection of my father." She retrieved a pack of cigarettes and a lighter. "I'd arrogantly thought I'd managed to be where I was all on my own." She lit a cigarette.

My interest was piqued. I leaned forward once more. "You need a husband?"

She took a deep drag off of her cigarette, nodded, and laid it all out for me. Halfway through I asked her to switch to English because her English was a thousand times better than my Russian.

I didn't want to outwardly show how shitty I thought it was that she'd need to marry a man just to retain what was already hers. I worked very hard to keep my face neutral and not show the outrage that was brewing just below the surface. She was about halfway through after she'd begun speaking in English, when I broke the seal. There was no way I could hold it in.

"Sebastian said that?"

"Da."

"And you think he's right?'

"Da."

"Sister." I reached over and squeezed her arm. "We can figure this out. You're not alone. You don't know my girls. We may not have the reach you need personally, but we can still put our heads together. Between all of us, we will figure out a plan. Trust me."

The intensity of emotion that ran over her face had me gripping her arm harder. "Do you need a hug?" I asked sincerely.

She laughed and I liked how it sounded. She continued to laugh so hard she had to grab her belly, and I swear I saw her cross her legs. It felt like I was witnessing something special.

"I can't remember the last time I laughed like that." Lydia wiped her eyes.

I looked away. If my asking if she wanted a hug made her laugh uncontrollably, she may not survive our tribe's level of affection. "Anytime you want a hug I've got one ready for you."

She smiled at me.

"I'm serious. Let's turn this thing around and meet up with my girls. The first thing you need to do is set up residence here. You don't want to go back there until you're safe."

"I appreciate your passion more than you know. But I don't want you and your friends involved in this." She leaned over and patted my knee. "My father isn't dead yet. I have a little bit of time to set some things in motion to survive him. As long as I do it now."

"I don't think you should go back to Russia until you have protection." I had a feeling it wouldn't go well for her. I couldn't explain where the feelings were coming from but my gut told me if she went back we wouldn't see her again. "I trust my gut. I'm an attorney. I was chased out of this country and stalked by a serial killer gang and I not only survived, but I've also thrived. I have a gut instinct that I listen to. Based on what you've shared with me, I don't think it's safe for you to go back." I looked at the men who rode in the front seat. I didn't know them. Could they be trusted?

She looked at me sideways. "Has Roman said anything?"

"Nope. Not one word. This is coming from my gut. Let me help you."

She looked out the window. The sun was beginning to come up. We'd been driving around town all night. "I'm not opposed to staying for a bit." She sniffed. "Maybe, I'll see how I feel about it. I fear I've lost my appetite in fighting the old ways for the new." She looked at me. "I'll talk to Aleks, and find out what he has available."

I smiled. "Come to my wedding and meet my friends."

She smiled back. "*Da.* I would love to."

24

Bonded

"Do you think this is smart? To leave him here like this... out cold?" Nadia asked her older sister.

"He's a big man, what can possibly hurt him out here?" Katrina replied with a shrug.

The three sisters looked around at the clearing they'd dragged their large cousin to. Slipping him the sedative that would knock him out was easy. He was busy arguing with their father about some woman from their homeland and wasn't paying any attention to what Katrina slipped into his drink.

Katrina tapped his heavy leg with the toe of her boot. "Admittedly, we may have over-sedated him."

"I don't think we should leave him here unconscious," Annika, the youngest of the three sisters murmured. "It would be terrible if something happened to him."

"He's *Romanov Stognafsky!*" Katrina reminded them, "He's Russian and not just any Russian, he is a Stognafsky! This is our tradition." She pounded her chest. "We were put in charge of the groom, were we not? And it's our duty to Mother Russia to see that some aspect of our traditional ways remains alive."

Nadia rolled her eyes and removed the envelope from her backpack, and gingerly pinned it to her slumbering cousin's jacket lapel. She'd begun to worry about her sister Katrina's plans about an hour east of Stockton. When they'd turned off onto an obscure forest road, she almost panicked. If she wasn't so afraid Katrina would leave her there too, she'd put her foot down. But her sister had become someone she could no longer predict, and that was frightening.

"I hope we made it easy enough for him to escape." Annika was sure this wasn't the best idea. Yes, it was traditional for a Russian groom to have to "buy" his way back to his bride through a set of tasks, it was how he proved his worthiness. But this seemed extreme. And so close to the wedding. If anything went wrong, he might not find his way back in time.

This felt kind of cruel. But much of what Katrina did these days felt mean and cruel. Annika's eyes flicked to Nadia's and held. A silent message passed between the two. They would have to keep an eye on this to make sure they weren't doing something that would hurt Romanov. He was good to them, and the girls loved Sydney, his soon-to-be wife, their soon-to-be cousin-in-law. She was to be their family.

"Couldn't we have made the scavenger hunt more fun and a little easier? Is all this really necessary?" Annika rarely spoke up against Katrina but this didn't feel right and Nadia was unusually tight-lipped.

"*Glupyy*," Katrina spat. "We placed arrows and left him a note. How much easier does it need to be? Let's go before he wakes up and all my hard work is ruined."

Annika and Nadia exchanged another look but followed the eldest sister to the parked vehicles without further argument. Annika climbed into her cousin Roman's large truck. Nadia and Katrina seated themselves in Katrina's SUV and the girls followed the narrow dirt road back to the main public road at a slow pace.

The vehicles stopped when the girls noticed the gates, which were wide open when they arrived at the main road, were now closed and had a chain and padlock securing them.

Annika opened the door, jumped down from the large truck, and walked back to her sister's car behind her.

"What do we do now?" She asked Katrina, gesturing toward the locked gates.

"Is it locked?"

"Yes."

Katrina pointed to the toolbox attached to the back of Roman's truck. "What do you think the odds are that *Romanov* would have something we could use to cut or break the chain, inside of that?"

Annika followed her line of sight and jumped into the back of the truck to access the toolbox. Sure enough, she found the key to the toolbox and retrieved a set of bolt cutters. She held them up and hooted. "Let the games begin!"

"Oh well, in for a dime, in for a dollar," Annika mumbled and hoped Romanov didn't freeze to death before he woke up.

Katrina leaned out of the SUV's window, "Park on the side so he can see it when he comes out. And put the key under the back passenger tire."

"What if he doesn't hike out this way?" Nadia mumbled.

Katrina's head whipped toward her sister. "Then he'll walk."

After parking the truck and placing the keys where she was instructed, Lydia stabbed the last small stake with a wooden arrow into the hard ground and jogged to the waiting car. "How will he know where to find the keys?"

Katrina shrugged her shoulders. "We left him clues."

Annika looked back at her cousin's large truck and wondered just how much trouble had Katrina gotten them into this time.

"You're in charge of my wedding games, Nadia," Annika whispered. Nadia nodded.

Katrina snickered.

Sadly, none of the girls saw the large sign that read;

"Keep Out! Endangered Species Wolf Preserve."

Or the new smaller sign below:

"Mating Season. Wolves may be Aggressive." Written in red letters. Nor did they know the Preserve Ranger had thanked his lucky stars that no one had found out that he'd left the gate wide open for an entire day.

Thankfully, the electronic tags still showed the wolves exactly where they were supposed to be. Behind the seven-foot gate.

25

That No Person

Roman groaned and tried to move off of whatever was digging into his back. Sydney had just paid a small fortune for this pain in the back bed, she was going to be pissed when he told her how shitty their expensive new mattress had become.

Funny, he didn't remember going to bed. He didn't even remember going home. Sydney deserved better than he was giving her at the moment.

He really was a fuckhead.

On that last thought, Roman attempted to roll over but couldn't seem to find his bearing. His head was fuzzy so he didn't think too much but instead rocked himself back and forth until he'd managed to work up enough steam to roll onto his front.

This unfortunately planted him face-first into dirt.

His eyes popped open and then closed immediately. He held his breath and waited until his head stopped pounding before he slowly tried opening them again. Yup, it was dirt and his face was covered in it.

Roman attempted to move his hands to his front and realized they were cuffed behind his back.

"What the fuck?" He growled and fought his restraints.

In one quick angry jerk, he managed to get himself in a seated position so he could take a look around and get his bearings.

"I'm in the fucking woods?" He asked aloud and blinked his eyes a few times just to make sure he was truly awake.

Convinced he was indeed awake, he pushed to his feet.

"Hello!" He spun around taking in his surroundings.

"Where... the fuck... am I?" Roman growled.

Roman pulled his wrists to his side, and pulled on his arms before wrestling once more with his restraints. Pretty quickly he realized they were not cuffs but zip ties. He relaxed with this bit of good news. Getting out of zip ties for a man of his size was not going to be nearly as difficult as getting out of cuffs would have been.

Looking around he scrambled to his knees and then pushed himself up into a standing position. From there he looked around and realized the forest he was in was fairly dense. He scanned for a thick branch, one that he could easily wedge his hands onto in order to pull down and break the zip tie.

It took a few tries and a few broken branches, but he finally managed on the third try to get a nice thick branch that he could get his hands over in order to pull down and break the zip tie. Once his arms were free, he rubbed his aching shoulders and realized that he had something pinned to his jacket. He ripped it off. Finding an envelope, he opened it and worked to get his eyes to focus. Rolling his head on his shoulders he read the note he'd retrieved.

"Dearest Romanov,

Happy engagement! Your fiancée thought it best to place us, your loving cousins, in charge of all things groom related regarding the wedding.

We thought it only appropriate to begin your journey as a true Russian groom by earning your way back to her.

If you're as smart as you think you are, the tasks set forth won't be difficult in the least, so pay attention.

In order to find the way out, you must leave the way you came.

Once you make your way to the beginning, you'll find an awaiting steed.

If you've made it this far, you're almost there. You should be able to locate your reins under the back left leg of the black beast."

The note was written on Stognafsky stationary and his three young cousins' signatures were below.

Damn it.

He patted his jacket and pants pockets. Gone. Everything was gone. His phone. His keys. His wallet. Everything.

God dammit.

Roman shook his head and looked around at the forest surrounding him, back down at the note, and then up to the sky.

"Really?" He asked the sky with his arms spread wide. He waited a beat and then put his hands on his hips. "I can't believe they did this to me."

He kicked one of the busted branches in front of him.

"How could they possibly think this was a good idea?" He kicked at a stone and as the pain traveled up his leg, he quickly realized it was a large rock buried mostly under the dirt.

"Agh!" He shouted and stumbled from the pain of breaking his toe.

"I'm going to wring their scrawny necks!" Roman shouted at the sky again and caught himself right before he stomped his injured foot.

He held himself as still as he'd ever been. If he didn't get himself in check he was never getting out of there. He'd already made his escape more difficult and painful by hurting his foot. He wiggled his toes and grimaced.

Definitely broken.

Rage surged back up. This was the last thing he needed. Lydia was not someone to leave unchecked. She would assume he was avoiding her and do something to get his attention. If that didn't work, she'd move to something more drastic. Roman knew in his gut this was going to put Sydney at risk.

He hung his head.

Shit, Sydney.

She was going to think he was blowing her off. If he hadn't been acting like a Neanderthal the last few days but instead had come clean with her, they wouldn't be in this mess now. All he wanted to do was marry his Angel and finally make them a whole family. He'd waited as she needed but after waiting so long, he needed her to move forward.

Maybe giving her the ultimatum wasn't the right thing to do. But dammit, he couldn't find a bit of regret. Fact was, he was damn tired of waiting. That woman could drag her feet like no one he'd ever known in his life.

He pushed those thoughts aside and focused on getting out of there before nightfall. Relief washed over him when he located a clear trail. When he saw the tire tracks, he actually cheered. As he followed his own truck tracks and it began to grow dark and cold, he dreamed of ways of torturing his young female cousins by kidnapping each of their grooms on their own wedding day.

If it was good for the goose... then it's going to be damn good for the gander. Or so they say.

He'd let the girls make that determination.

26

Shall Put Asunder

"I'm going to murder them!" Roman shouted as the largest of the wolves nipping at his leather heel. He was solidly up a tree. Literally.

The wolf pack had started tracking him shortly after he left the site where he'd been dumped and began following the truck tracks out of the forest. He could feel something pacing him but he couldn't figure out what it was. He'd begun to suspect his cousins were "hunting" him as part of the "prank". That was until he rounded a corner and through the dense forest got a look at the deadly creature. The biggest damn silver wolf he'd ever seen.

"Mother Fu…." Roman shouted before he hightailed it up the closest tree… one he hoped would hold his weight. His jacket ripped, then his shirt, and he swore he felt the seam split in the ass of his trousers. He could give a shit about his clothes, because the wolf had chased him and was now scratching at the tree howling and growling only inches below.

Suddenly there was another wolf, then another, and then another, until the entire pack, he presumed, was below him, and surrounding the tree growling and howling.

Roman glanced around at his situation. He certainly wasn't thrilled with where he'd currently found himself.

"I'm literally up a fucking tree," he growled. "Sydney is going to lose her shit when I tell her about this." Just thinking about her had dueling effects on his psyche. On one side, when he conjured her image in his mind it calmed his soul. She didn't know exactly how much he needed her or how deep it ran for him. On the other hand, thinking about his bride brought anxiety because she was going to be so freaking pissed... and he was worried about her safety.

The tree seemed sturdy, but he didn't want to test the branches, so he tried to remain as still as possible while he attempted to get comfortable. He had a feeling he was going to be up there a while.

"I guess I should just be happy it's not bear season." Roman ignored the wolves so they would calm. It took some time but one by one they laid down under the tree. His eye caught the torn jacket pocket on one of his favorite suits.

"Dammit! This was my favorite suit." Sydney liked it. He knew this because she cupped his ass every single time he wore it.

"Military school is looking better and better. I wonder how hard it would be to talk Aleks into it. Those girls are a menace." Roman shook his head. He knew the oldest was the instigator especially since she was the oldest, the other two probably just fell into line. But they still made the decision to leave him out there.

Him.

Roman.

Their favorite cousin... supposedly!

He'd make them pay. Each one of them and they'd never see it coming.

Roman's view shifted back to the noisy wolves. Surely, they'd get hungry enough and leave for easier prey sometime soon.... wouldn't they? Roman's eyes rolled to the sky... that is unless he was the easier prey.

He tried to think back to when everything went so wrong. His life is going so well.

Why now?

When he was finally getting Sydney!

He had the woman of his dreams within his grasp and it seemed like the entire earth's population was doing everything in its power to keep them apart. The woman he had literally dreamed of for six long agonizing years.

His Angel.

His.

And she was *finally* becoming his wife.

Why? Why on the cusp of their union would everything fall apart? Bit by bit it seemed to be chipping away at his control. If something didn't give soon he was going to blow his gasket. A quiet solo wedding for two sounded just perfect to him. But for her? For her he'd move heaven and earth to give her what she wanted. What she needed. As long as it happened soon.

Roman looked around.

How had he let things get so far off course? How had he let this happen?

27

Our Commitment

Once the wolf pack grew bored, they left. It was early morning and Roman's muscles were sore with more than a couple of his limbs numb. He thought for sure they'd move on once they grew hungry.

Nope.

It was freezing out and while California weather wasn't nearly as frigid as other places in the country, it still dipped well below what was comfortable for humans. Turns out the wolves took a liking to the security of the large tree - the same one he was up - and spent the night mating under it; which was a lot more violent than he'd ever realized. Their howling was ear-piercing and set Roman's teeth on edge. But that wasn't even the worst of it...the worst was the pack fighting over and ripping apart two small unlucky critters.

Nature at its finest. Any other time this would be interesting. Now it was sickening.

The pack moved to sleep off their night of debauchery ... yep, you guessed, under the same tree. Which left Roman to shiver and cling in the cold of the night. Good thing he had a layer of fat on him. He had Isabella to thank. This was also encouraging because that meant he wouldn't have to think twice about having seconds. He could absolutely justify it for the sake of survival.

Roman shifted his hip and made one last sweep of the landscape before deciding to call the all-clear. Now to brace his stiff muscles for the impact of landing.

He hesitated. He'd hate to end up like one of those poor tiny souls that had been the wolves' dinner. On a deep sigh and a prayer to the Lord above, he allowed his weary muscles to release for the first time in many hours and braced for impact. Hitting the ground didn't hurt nearly as much as he thought it would, probably because half of his body was numb, but he believed in being thankful for the gifts when they presented themselves.

"This is my fucking karma for being a super dick to Sydney." He scavenged around the brush until he located a small solid log that was long enough he could swing and inflict damage before whatever it was he was swinging at could get too close enough to hurt him. He rested it up against his shoulder with a firm grip, holding it like a batter stepping up to the plate.

"Angel is going to be so pissssssed at me." Talking to himself seemed like a good way to work through some of his frustration within. Being stuck up the tree gave him time to reflect on how big of a jerk he'd been to Sydney. If he'd only been honest with her from the beginning none of this would have happened. Freezing his ass off made him realize how good his life was and how little he had to complain about. What a fucking fool he'd been. What was he thinking giving Sydney an ultimatum? No one would be able to convince him after this that he'd done the right thing. He should have planned a romantic wedding in Paris and brought all of her girls along. Making her choose?

What the hell was wrong with him?

Well, he wouldn't make this mistake again. He'd never push her to do something she wasn't ready for. Especially use her girls against her

- which is what he did and knew how it would prompt her to move her rear. It wasn't right or fair. It's not how you treat the most perfect woman in the world. It wasn't and he was ashamed of his actions.

This was his just dessert. If he hadn't pushed her to do something she wasn't ready for, he wouldn't have spent a freezing night up a tree.

Roman closed his eyes. Truth be told, he was worried she was waiting to tie the knot because she wasn't totally sure he was the man for her. He should have been more patient. All the reasons she'd postponed the wedding were legitimate. Sydney hadn't been looking for reasons to postpone... they just kept finding her... them.

He shifted his cold legs to try and bring blood circulation back to his hindquarters.

"Well, I might still be stuck out here. But those girls are going to have their asses handed to them as soon as I get a hold of them." It was freezing.

The girls he once thought were sweet sheltered debutantes were clearly hideous gremlins in disguise. What had happened to the sweet girls he'd known... and trusted? And what had he done to deserve this kind of treatment right before what was supposed to be the happiest day of his and Sydney's life?

"I'm going to wring their necks," he growled.

Aleks was going to have to do something about them. This was unacceptable behavior.

Roman barked a burst of laughter that wasn't funny. His uncle probably had no clue what little monsters his daughters had become. They batted their lovely eyes at their father and he gave them whatever they wanted.

"He can bet his ass I am going to let him know just how far south they've gone! What little criminals, they've become!" He was law enforcement for fucks sake. If they'd do this to him, they would do this to anyone. Roman slowed his pace. Maybe Aleks knows and put them up to this. He could be trying to delay the wedding in order to give Lydia time to arrive.

Another thought washed over him. What if Lydia has already gone after Sydney as a last resort to stop the wedding?

No, that didn't add up. Aleks loved Sydney. Even his men loved her. Roman growled. Sebastian loved her a little too much. He nodded to himself. Sebastian may make Roman uncomfortable but he could count on him to keep Sydney safe. It wouldn't matter what Aleks said, what command he gave, Sebastian would never raise a hand against her and he'd never let anyone else harm her either. This at least was something he was sure of.

The big brute had mistakenly left bruises on Sydney during their first encounter. It had haunted the deadly enforcer and he'd suffered from what he'd done. Roman felt confident he wouldn't lay hands on her again.

The scared and battle-wise *Bratva* enforcer sacrificed his own life to save Sydney's, he knew then and there the man would do it again and again if called on.

His girl just had that effect on people. She worked so hard to care for those who had no one without realizing she was gathering an army at her back along the way.

"Damn." He missed his Angel.

28

To One Another

Roman spotted his black truck just on the other side of a large locked gate. Relief washed over him; he was going to actually make it out.

The sun was coming up and if he wasn't mistaken today was actually his wedding day.

He let out a little cheer and threw his fist at the sky in celebration. As he made it around the bend, he noticed a ranger truck had pulled in just between him and his truck with its door popped open. A ranger jumped out.

"Well, howdy there Mister. You know this here is federal land, right?"

"Officer, thank God. You are a sight for sore eyes!" Roman began walking quicker toward the Ranger.

"Well now fella, just hold it right there. Don't come any closer." The Ranger reached for his holstered sidearm.

Roman stopped walking and put his arms up. "I'm an officer of the law. I don't have my wallet or my badge on me right now. Someone took them and dumped me out here. But, if you look behind you, my truck is just past the gate. Run the plate and you'll come up with my identification."

"I said stop right there and don't you come any closer. In fact, I want you to keep your hands above your head and lay down on your stomach."

"You've got to be kidding me." Roman growled while he did as he was told. The last thing he wanted was to be murdered by some freaked-out park ranger on his wedding day. Wouldn't that just be his luck? Roman complied and found his face in the dirt for the second time in less than a day.

"Hey man, run the plates on my truck and you'll see who I am. I'm in law enforcement, too. A detective with the sheriff's department."

"You stay just like that, don't move. I'll see who you are. We'll figure this out, in the meantime, I'm going to handcuff you and put you in the back of my car. No funny business now and we will have this settled up one way or another, easy breezy."

"Easy breezy, hunh?" Roman didn't think anything about this entire situation had been easy breezy. His muscles were sore. He needed a shower ... and his bed ... and he wanted Sydney in it with him.

"How the fuck," Roman mumbled, "did I end up here?" Of course, he was stuck with Barney Fife. Roman was probably the first arrest he'd ever made.

Ranger Fife took Roman's hands and gently placed a set of cuffs on him. Then he had a hell of a time trying to pick a man up who probably weighed twice as much as he did.

Finally, Roman, after he'd had just about enough, barked, "Before you rip my arms out of their sockets do you think I could roll to my side and stand up on my own?"

"I suppose that'd be fine. No funny business." Roman rolled to his side and pushed to his feet in one economical motion. As he rose to his full height Ranger Fife stepped closer and Roman towered over him.

"What indication have I given you that I am going to resist or give you any grief at all?" Roman's patience was running out. "I'll tell you one thing." Roman would be looking into the Ranger training program and also why this guy was allowed to roam free while armed. "I miss my wedding because you're dicking around, I'll not only take your job, I'll make sure you never work in law enforcement again." He leaned in. "That's a promise."

How the fuck did he end up here and when did his life change so drastically that everything went against him? First, his own cousins left him out to rot with a bunch of wolves, and now the guy he thought was going to rescue him, had him in handcuffs and was about to take him to jail ... on his wedding day. What in the world has Roman done to deserve this kind of karma?

"Look here, mister. I'm just doing my job. If you are who you say you are, what would you do? You come stumbling out of the sanctuary looking like you've been wrestling with a tree all night." The small ranger placed his hands on his belt. "Another thing, what in the living hell were you doing in that sanctuary? Don't you know the wolves are in a second heat and they are most aggressive when they're feeling frisky." The ranger wiggled his brows.

Roman nodded. "They tore a rabbit to pieces and humped all night."

Ranger Fife's mouth dropped open. "You saw them?"

"The pack chased me up that tree you mentioned earlier. They carried on underneath it where I spent the night... in the tree... all night. Hence my appearance."

The look the ranger was giving Roman had him shuffling his feet. The two of them stared at each other for a few moments.

"Do you want to take me to the station? Or even better run my plates and let me go?" He rolled his shoulders as much as the cuffs would allow. "It's my wedding day, man."

The ranger moved to Roman's truck. "You just stay right there and hold your horses."

"Where am I going with my hands cuffed?"

The ranger spent a bit of time at the truck and as he walked back toward Roman he said, "Well, I suppose if the wolves thought you were good enough to spend the night with, you're all right with me."

Roman laughed. "That's what convinced you? The wolves?"

Ranger Fife set about unlocking the cuffs on Roman's wrists. "Well, your truck did come back identifying you and collaborating with you. Partner, you've no idea how lucky you are. Those wolves are a rare wolf breed. One that we've been trying to rebuild the population on for years. We're hoping the pups will be born in late spring. I'm afraid it doesn't look good for them."

"What does that mean?" Roman rubbed his wrists.

"That means sir, that you had the honor of watching the last pack in the world of that particular breed, we don't have high hopes for their survival."

"Are you kidding me? They were going at it all night long."

"Really?" That little tidbit perked the ranger's mood.

"Oh yeah. You need to get cameras up around here."

"We don't have the funding I'm afraid."

Roman smiled for the first time in many days. "You do now."

"We do?"

"Yep. Listen, I'll make you a deal. You get me to my wedding on time and I'll get you a few approved cameras out here. And I'll recount everything I saw with descriptions of the wolves. Deal?"

"Oh yes, mister! That's a deal."

Ranger Fife took Roman's hand and shook it with the gleeful enthusiasm of a six-year-old on Christmas morning.

"How about we get you married!"

Roman smiled again. "How about we do that."

29

With Reassurance

"Girl, you better pace yourself. It's not even two and that's your third drink." Jenna snatched the customized shot glass from Becca's hand and set it on the bar.

"I've had one whiskey, one Champagne, and one vodka. It would be rude to leave one of them out." She crossed her arms. "If you were as good a friend as you claim you'd be taste testing too. Gotta make sure everything is up to snuff."

"Up to snuff?"

"Yeah, you know. On par." Jenna didn't respond. "Good enough, alright? I had to make sure the liquor served was good enough for our girl and Roman."

Sloane approached her friends. "Are we drinking? I'm in."

"Just tasting." Jenna wasn't feeling the excuse Becca laid down.

"Well, I'm the chemist." Sloane turned to the person setting up the glasses around the large ice sculpture. "I'll have a shot."

"What would you like, ma'am?"

"Ma'am?" Sloane looked offended.

"Yeah, it's one of those parties. Just go with it," Becca mumbled to

Sloane without taking her eyes off Jenna. "The vodka is good but the whiskey bar is fantastic!"

"Yes, please!" Sloane threw back the shot of vodka offered and the two moved off toward the whiskey bar.

"Just don't get drunk!" Jenna shouted after her friends who she was certain were going to be drunk as a skunk well before the wedding began.

"Jenna!" Terra yelled and hurried over. "I just got an alert that Sydney has been kidnapped!"

"What? When?" Jenna quickly closed the gap between the two women so they weren't shouting. Too late, however, Sloane and Becca spun on their heels and rushed back to them.

"What's happening?"

"Has anyone called Roman?"

"I don't know what's happening. And yes, they've been trying to get Roman for over an hour."

"An hour?" Becca yelled. "How long has she been gone?"

"The camera showed a man and a woman. The man put Sydney over his shoulder at what appeared to be at the woman's instruction." Terra, who was normally our cool and calm friend, was rattled.

"That Russian bitch!" Becca shouted. Terra nodded her head in agreement.

"What do we do now?" Sloane was newer to the group and tended to follow the lead instead of taking it on herself.

Terra paced up and down the small walkway the ladies were standing on. "We need to get Cabe involved without alerting Isabella. She has to keep the food preparations going."

"Why? If we don't have a couple, there can't be a wedding." Becca looked around the small group. "We should call it off."

"No!" Terra, Jenna, and Sloane said at once.

Becca put her hands up. "Why would we have a wedding without the bride and groom?"

"Because we have nearly a hundred people arriving on Christmas Eve and we aren't turning them away, regardless of what happens with Roman and Sydney." Terra pointed at Becca. "Do you hear me?"

"I got you. I promise I won't say a word." She pretended to zip her mouth shut and threw the make-believe key over her shoulder. "I swear." Becca lowered her voice, "Sydney was worried about Roman's," she made air quotes with her fingers. "betrothed doing something to stop the wedding."

"It's not a good sign that they're both missing."

"Bitch, I agree," Becca said.

"Don't call her bitch." Jenna missed the eye roll Becca replied with. "What time are hair and makeup supposed to be here?"

"One hour."

"Okay, they can start on us." Jenna was in "fix it" mode. "I've already got the dresses in the house ready to go." She looked around the finished grounds where the wedding was to take place. "Everything looks so gorgeous. It'd be a serious shame if the wedding doesn't happen."

"If the wedding doesn't happen today does that mean Roman is making her go to Vegas?"

"If he does, I'm going too." Terra smiled at her friends. "We've earned it."

"I'm going to find Cabe." Jenna spun on her heel and was off.

"Remember don't alert Isabella!" Beca shouted after her. Sloane slapped a hand over Becca's mouth but it was too late.

"Don't alert Isabella about what?" Isabella asked as she approached the group.

"Oh, shit..." this time Jenna didn't shush Becca's language... she agreed with it.

30

Acceptance

Even though Lydia said she would take me to Francesca's, we had to stop first and grab a change of clothes for her. She'd explained that while she was forfeiting her rights to Roman, he still deserved to see what he was missing out on. I squinted at her but let that roll, since she was still in agreement, I didn't want to do anything that might change her mind.

"Hey, I know this place. Aleks lives here. You're taking me to Aleks?"

"*Da*. My things are here for the time being. I'll only be a little bit."

I giggled. I didn't mean to but I have a condition that when I get stressed, I laugh and giggle. It's usually misinterpreted. Roman was the only one who really knew how stressed I was if I started giggling.

But the situation was almost absurd. She was worried about how she was going to look on my wedding day...while holding me up getting ready... again, for my wedding day.

The audacity.

"Any help she thought she was getting from me is out the door," I mumbled.

The door popped open and I was pulled from the car. Mind you, I was wearing the same clothes I'd been wearing from the day before, and dragged into Aleks home. This was reminiscent of the first time I'd visited Aleks' home. Only that time it had been Sebastian who dragged me through the door.

I doubt there was going to be a big sexy Roman charging in to save me this time. I had a feeling that if I wanted to make it to my wedding I was gonna have to get myself there, but first, I needed to figure out a way to get out of Lydia's clutches. It's not that I was mad at her, and it's not that I didn't feel bad either, but this was my wedding day dammit. I deserved not to be kidnapped on my damn wedding day. I'd already not slept all night, hadn't had a shower, and now I was supposed to wait on this bimbo? I didn't think so.

"Little warrior, what are you doing here? Isn't today your wedding day?" Sebastian stopped in front of me with confusion written all over his face.

"Indeed, it is my wedding day. But, instead of getting ready for what is supposed to be the happiest day of my life, I'm stuck here with a freaked-out Russian assassin who thinks my Roman is supposed to be her groom." I patted Sebastian's chest. "Now don't get it wrong, Lydia is supposed to take me," she says" to my wedding. But only after she looks her best. Tell me what's wrong with this?"

"Does Roman know where you are?"

"No! Roman does not!" I was starting to get hot under the collar. How many times was I gonna have to say it? Over and over again, that this was *my* wedding day and I haven't been able to see my groom or speak to him in two days? It seemed like nobody was listening to me.

So, I raised my voice.

"Today is my wedding day. I don't know where my groom is. I've been kidnapped by a Russian assassin who wanted to marry my husband and now you're questioning me about where he is? I don't freaking know where he is!" I took a deep breath. "Do you think you can give me a ride to the 4 F? Please?"

"*Da.* I'll get you over there right now. Don't worry *little warrior, Romanov* would never leave you standing at the altar."

"*Oh, Lord Almighty!* I know he wouldn't on purpose. But, let's be honest here, I was just kidnapped by a Russian assassin, who's to say he hasn't been kidnapped too or worse!" The last thing I wanted to do was freak out. I calmed myself. "Look, can you give me a ride or not?"

"*Da.* I'll pull the car around."

"Not without me you aren't. Someone is going to come along and throw me in another damn car and head in the opposite direction!"

"Follow me. I'll call Aleks and alert him on the way."

"Where do you think you're going?" Lydia stepped through the doorway just as we were heading towards the car. "Especially with my little treasure, Sebastian?"

"Please... please take me to Francesca's." I grabbed Sebastian's arm and hugged it while I pleaded. "I'm not gonna have enough time to get ready if you don't get me over there now."

He put his hand over mine which was still gripping his arm. "You are with me now. You don't need to worry about anybody taking you anywhere else."

"Sydney, I thought we came to an agreement. You little traitor, you were so convincing."

"Look Lydia, I'm still on your side. I totally get where you're coming from, but you kept me from getting ready for my wedding so you could get ready for... once again *my* wedding... you understand how twisted that is right? And that's after keeping me up all night. The night before my wedding. You do understand that this is not how friendships are made and kept... right?"

"*Da.* I do understand. And this is why I don't have any friends." She shook her head and if I wasn't freaking out about getting to my wedding I might have time to feel sorrier for her. But given that she had kidnapped me and instead of getting me where I'd been begging to go for hours...I had little room left for compassion. "Give me another chance to show you I can do this."

She offered me her hand and like a fool I took it. She pulled me away from Sebastian and shoved me toward her henchman. "I'm sorry old friend. I need to be the one who rides in on the white horse and delivers the princess. It's how I shall redeem myself."

"This is not how these people work. You can't strong-arm them and have it go your way. Or any way." Sebastian stepped right in front of Lydia so she was forced to look up at him. "Return her to me now or I will take her and you won't like what that costs you."

"Sebastian, my old friend, and confidant. How could you betray me in this manner?"

"I warned you not to do this. I warned you that I would choose her over you if you made me. Now you're making me." He threw his shoulders back to ready for whatever he was planning to do. Whatever it was was enough to make Lydia back down.

"Release her." Once the command left her mouth the grip the henchman had on my arm released.

"Let me take her. Let me be the one to deliver her."

Sebastian looked at me and then back at Lydia, then at her henchmen, and then back at me.

"Get in my car, Sydney." The words hadn't fully left his mouth when I sprinted to the car, jumped in, closed the door behind me, and locked it.

Then I unlocked it and locked it again for good measure. I didn't know what they were talking about but I sure as heck understood what body language was displayed as Sebastian berated Lydia and her henchmen. They must've come to some agreement because pretty quickly Lydia was doing the talking and Sebastian was nodding his head like he was in agreement. I could only pray that the agreement was not about me leaving this vehicle and that somebody was coming to drive me to Francesca's ranch.

Finally, Sebastian, Lydia, and the henchmen headed toward the car. Frantically, I scrambled to make sure all four doors were locked.

"Unlock the door, Sydney." Sebastian knocked on the window.

"Nope." I shook my head. "I'm not opening it until you promise me that you're going to take me straight to Francesca's. On Aleks life, you promise me."

"*Da*, I promised you. No need for extremes. I will always keep my promises to you. Lydia is coming with us, but I am driving." He tapped his chest and then held up the key fob showing that he could get in anytime he wanted.

I gave Sebastian the stink eye, then gave Lydia the same stink eye, and lastly turned it to her henchman who could have cared less. Only after I felt they all got my point, did I hit the unlock button. Lydia and her henchman climbed in the back, Sebastian got behind the wheel, and off we went.

I could only pray they were taking me to Francesca's. I felt pretty confident after a bit. I'd kept a sharp eye on where we were going and so far we were on the right road heading in the right direction. I relaxed, even more, when we turned down Francesca's street, and I almost cried when we turned onto Francesca's driveway. All of my girls were there, all their cars were lined up. I had to know they were freaking out.

The scary thing? Roman's car was not there. My stomach dropped. Where was he?

I opened the door before the car fully stopped but waited...as soon as we came to a stop I jumped and ran towards the gazebo next to the pond where the wedding was set up.

I don't know what came over me. I just knew that I needed my girls, I needed to find my Roman and I needed this day to be over. I was seriously rethinking the validity of taking the jet to Vegas and blowing off this whole disaster.

I screamed and all the heads turned toward me. I saw the girls, they saw me, and read my face while taking in the fact that I was running full speed away from the car I'd just arrived in.

I don't run. Like I tell Jenna every year; Not. A. Runner. But I was running like my britches were on fire.

Becca slammed the glass she was holding down. The joy and elation that I felt when I saw Becca running towards me was over the top. I laughed not because I was stressed out but because it was so ridiculous everything that had happened. Then I went from elated to confused when Becca, who I thought was running towards me, streaked right past me.

Yep, the girl kept on going. I felt a slight breeze as she rushed past.

I slowed down to turn and watch as Becca screamed in what can only be described as a blood-curdling banshee voice and tackled the perfectly coiffed Lydia to the ground. Lydia was tall and curvy; sophisticated. Becca was short and petite, a rancher. Tiny was a great word to describe Becca... as long as you didn't take her personality into consideration. Once you got even a taste of all that was Becca, she didn't appear small any longer.

To put it bluntly, Becca was larger than life. As she proved by attacking a Russian assassin nearly twice her size on my wedding day.

My breath caught.

Lydia's henchmen jumped on top of Becca, who was on top of Lydia. Becca was flailing her arm screaming and yelling curse words. It didn't appear that Becca actually landed any blows because Lydia appeared unconcerned about Becca swinging on her. Lydia was too preoccupied with keeping her hair from getting messed up to worry about what Becca was up to. Didn't say much about Becca's abilities.

At this point I'd stopped running and the other girls had caught up to me. Stella slid her arm around my waist and laid her head on my shoulder.

We watched as Sebastian pulled Becca back with an arm around her waist. Until she managed to get away. He wrangled her once more, but she wiggled out of his hold again and again. He didn't seem overly motivated to contain Becca.

One had to stop and watch these kinds of things. It was an unwritten rule. There was no way to avoid the train wreck. And to be honest, I can't tell you I didn't enjoy watching Becca tackle the perfectly groomed Lydia to the ground. Especially after she made me wait to get ready for my own wedding. Yeah, it stung. I didn't think I was gonna get over it anytime soon... in a year... maybe two. Even if I decided to help her in the long run, which I was pretty certain I was, she had a lot to make up for before that was going to happen.

I know what you're thinking; that I'm nuts to have anything to do with her. But let's face it, she's a Russian princess/ladyboss assassin and *she* needed *my* help. If that wasn't a boost to the old ego, I didn't know what was.

"Damn if you don't worry me, sister, the trouble that finds you." Jenna closed in on my left and leaned against me. We stood and watched as this pile of people seemed to be fighting, but not really injuring one another. I had the feeling Lydia could have snuffed Becca in a second but simply didn't want to.

I had a twinge of wanting to help Becca but I also didn't want to move any closer to the people who had kidnapped me. You know, self-preservation and all that.

Terra stepped closer. "Here's the thing, we don't really have time for this." She waved her perfectly manicured fingers at the scene.

Sebastian had straightened and was watching us. I looked to Terra, who was watching Sebastian, and back to Sebastian who was stiff as a board like he'd forgotten what was going on around him.

Interesting information to file away for later. But right now, I had a wedding to get ready for and I hadn't had a wink of sleep all night.

I leaned toward Terra. "By all that is holy, please ask that big gorgeous Russian to stop this madness so I can get married." Terra looked surprised and I swear her face turned red.

"Why would I ask him?" She was acting like they hadn't been playing googly eyes for the last five minutes.

I moved to stand facing her with my back to the mayhem. I took her hands in mine.

"I love you. But we don't have time for me to convince you that you have influence over that guy." I pointed with my thumb behind me. "I need you to simply ask him to do this one thing, without thinking too much about it." I had a thought. "Be the event coordinator I know you are." I decided it was going to be too hard to convince her of his affection. Quicker to appeal to her business ego. Much more diplomatic.

And it worked.

"Of course." She stepped around me and assessed the pile of people who were trying not to hurt each other. Or more accurately, two people trying not to hurt one person who was trying, however unsuccessfully, to hurt them.

She marched straight to Sebastian, his eyes trained on her with every step that brought her closer to him. This might be the first time that she'd approached him of her own volition.

"We should get you in the house honey." Jenna took my arm.

"Hold on. I want to see this." I grabbed her hand so she would witness it with me. As you know I trust my gut. It rarely lets me down. I could feel this moment was something big and we should be there to witness it.

Jenna, who also trusted my gut, stopped and enjoyed the thick sexual tension that swirled around Sebastian while he watched Terra.

"Dayum." Jenna giggled. "Go on with your badass self, sister."

Terra stopped next to Sebastian. He took a step closer and bent over her, affording them a sphere of intimacy.

Jenna and I sighed in unison. We watched Terra look up into his ruggedly handsome face.

And then he smiled.

A full-on white, dimple-creating, sexy-as-sin smile.

"Oh my gosh," Jenna whispered. I squeezed her arm as we leaned on each other.

We could see Terra speaking to him. His eyes were glued to her mouth. Before we knew it, she spun on her heel and marched right back the way she came, where we were watching her interact with her new boyfriend.

She saw our smirks and returned one of her own. "What are you doing? Get your rear in the house and get in the shower!"

Yes, that sounded like a wonderful idea. I wanted a shower so much.

"I need my bag. It got left at the house."

"I'll go get it now." Jenna turned to leave but I stopped her. "Grab Agatha too, please. Her carrier is in my bedroom closet, on the floor right when you open the door. My bag is packed and sitting on the bed."

She hugged me and left before I could give her any more directions.

"Wait, has anyone heard from Roman?"

Terra leaned her head towards mine. "Cabe is looking for him," she said quietly.

"Cabe?" My stomach dropped. "He hasn't found him yet? What's happening?" I was totally freaking out from this news and the fact that I hadn't slept was starting to wear on me. My coping skills were a bit saturated at the moment.

Before long, Sebastian had the henchman pulled off of Becca. Then he pulled Becca off of Lydia, and her henchman helped her stand up.

Becca stopped fighting Sebastian and as a group, we turned to watch as Cabe's car, Laird's truck, and a park ranger vehicle raced up Francesca's driveway with Lucas hot on their tail riding his motorcycle.

I watched the caravan and all the dust they were kicking up all over Francesca's gorgeous while poinsettias and the flocked trees and rage bubbled up.

"That's it!" I marched toward the offending vehicles with every intention of giving them a loud *what for*… and boy was I planning to give it to them good.

31

Love

The caravan skid to a stop kicking up more dust than they had generated all the way down the driveway. I was fit to be tied and madder than a hornet.

My face felt beat red. I know my hair was big and frizzy. I was stomping in two-day-old clothes with zero sleep on my damn wedding day. Literally, everything that could go wrong had just about gone wrong. Whoever this was, they were going to get an earful if I had anything to say about it.

And I sure did have something to say.

Imagine my surprise when the man of my dreams popped out of the passenger side of that ranger's vehicle. He looked worse than I did.

His suit was torn, his pants were torn, his face was dirty, he had something in his hair and he had a giant scratch running down his cheek.

He was the most beautiful thing I've ever seen in my entire life. My angry stomp quickly turned into a joyful skip and I skipped my way right into that man's open arms.

I ignored Terra who was screaming at me "Not to let him see me".

I ignored Jenna who also tried to get me to come back. I ignored all of them, nothing was going to stop me from jumping into that man's arms.

Which is exactly what I did. He went back on a foot to brace himself for my impact. I wrapped my legs around his hips and my arms around his neck and not one fucking person was prying me off of him.

I didn't have to worry because he wrapped his arms around me and held onto me almost as tight as I was holding onto him.

I laughed and cried and kissed his face.

I held my hands against his cheeks and looked into his eyes. "Where the hell have you been, baby?"

"You wouldn't believe me if I told you." Judging by the way he looked he was probably right.

"I hate to be a party pooper. But now that everyone is here, and we are all clearly safe, if you don't get in the shower, you're not going to get your hair and makeup done in time. You're not going to make the wedding." Terra put her hands on her hips.

I kissed my groom's gorgeous mouth.

"She's right, let's get this damn thing done, I just want to be married to you. I'm glad I don't have to do this again. I wish I would've just chosen Vegas."

"I'm sorry baby. This isn't what I wanted for us. I'll make it up to you on the honeymoon."

"If you'd just offered to take us along to Vegas we could've already had this done by now!" Becca shouted.

Roman looked at her and came back to me. "What's she talking about?"

"Becca is pissed off we aren't going to Vegas. She's just saying that if the girls had been invited there was a bigger chance we might have taken advantage of the Vegas wedding proposition."

"Are you kidding me?" Roman hit his forehead. "If I had known that,

I would've changed the parameters. Haven't you heard of negotiating? You're an attorney!"

"Really?" I dropped my legs, my feet hitting the ground.

I tried to pull back but Roman secured his arms around me and pulled my body against his chest.

"Do you want to get married today or not? Because my friends and I went through a lot of trouble to make this happen."

I made a sweeping motion of the white sparkling Christmas wedding that my friends had creatively brought to life. I held my finger up and began counting down.

"It's Christmas Eve. My wedding day. I haven't slept at all. I've been kidnapped, chased, and again…I haven't had any sleep. Did I mention that? I'd like to get this done so I can go to bed."

I knew better. I should've been paying attention. The only excuse that came to mind is that I hadn't had any sleep, and I'd been very emotional the last few days… weeks.

Really, all the fighting with Roman, it just wasn't us. I should've been paying closer attention to his reaction when I was running my little rant down. If I had been, I would've noticed that his stance had changed and he'd grown rigid. His energy had shifted.

Nope, I was more consumed with my own traumatic day …and also how ripe my guy was.

"You stink. Terra's right. You need a shower."

He looked down at me. For a moment he remained silent, seemingly came to an internal decision, and smiled in a way that made his eyes twinkle.

I recognized that grin. It looked a lot like the one Sebastian had given Terra. Only mine was even better, richer, deeper.

The smile that said everything I needed to hear, without a spoken word. My eyes filled and chills ran over my skin.

I popped up on my tippy toes and gave him a swift kiss on his plump sexy mouth. "Will you marry me?" I whispered.

He gave me a half grin. "The sooner the better."

That was the cue Terra had been waiting for.

"All right you lovebirds. Luckily for you, I'm not superstitious. But, you," she pointed at Roman. "Need to go get showered, cause big fella you might be easy on the eyes... but you stink to high heaven." She turned to me. "And you need to go get showered and get yourself ready for hair and makeup," She clapped her hands. "We are *way* behind schedule."

I gave my big guy a tight squeeze and a kiss on the cheek.

Then, I did as I was told. I'm here to tell you that shower was the best thing that happened to me so far that day, well, after seeing Roman.

I breezed through hair and makeup while the girls bustled around me. Francesca gave us each a beautiful pearl ring with rough-cut rubies. We had a short moment where we remembered Raquel and Antonio until Isabella got mad. She thought we were going to ruin our makeup so we had to stop talking about them. We agreed we would reminisce about them later when we could ruin our makeup and no one would care.

The beautiful dress that Jenna had made for me was a winter white sophisticated satin I'd seen earlier. But once the sleeves and train were attached it was no longer beautiful ... Now it was drop-dead gorgeous, straight to the floor with long sleeves and white fur on the cuffs. It was off the shoulder with white fur that trimmed the collar. My train was about three feet and the bottom of the dress was trimmed in the same arctic white fur.

Simple, classy, elegant.

"I'm trying not to cry, sister. But this dress is exactly what I pictured. How did you know?"

Jenna smiled softly. "It's how I've always seen you. Raquel and I would talk about who would look right in a white dress when they got married and we agreed that yours should be simple, classy, sassy, and elegant because you, my friend, are the epitome of sassy elegance."

"Great. There goes my mascara." Becca shouted it from behind us. "This is why I can't wear makeup. You bitches are always making me cry."

"Stop calling us bitches." Jenna smiled and put her arm around Becca. "You wouldn't have it any other way. We keep you human."

There was a knock at the door and a flurry of movement as the girls made sure it wasn't Roman coming to steal me away. It wasn't, it was Sebastian that wanted a word with me alone.

"I want to give you one last chance to change your mind. If you need, I can get you out of here and keep you safe." He was awkward and I almost felt like he didn't really have his heart in it but he felt it was his duty to give me a way out and to make sure this was truly what I wanted. This was his manly way of being a good girlfriend. I knew it in my heart. But he didn't want that for me I could tell, he wanted me with Roman. He didn't have to worry, I wanted me with Roman too.

"You're such a sweet man. I'm so glad I met you and that you're part of my family now. But Roman is the man I love, he's the man I see myself with... he's the one I want to grow old with."

For the second time that day, I popped up on my tippy toes and planted a kiss on a big Russian man's cheek. But this time it wasn't the man I was going to be married to, it was a man who cared enough to put himself out to make sure I was okay. And knowing that, I knew I'd always be okay. How could it go wrong with so many people rooting for us?

The girls were already in their beautiful dresses and we were having pictures taken when Francesca's daughter arrived to let her know that Laird was waiting for her at the arbor. That was a relief because Laird was the one officiating the ceremony. And honestly, I hadn't even thought about asking if he was there yet! We'd already signed all the documents needed beforehand. We would only have to put our signatures on them after the ceremony.

With one final snap from the photographer and love all around, Francesca went running out the door with her daughter. She said she'd meet us at the arbor and blew a kiss.

Chills ran over my skin as I heard the music start up outside. Francesca had hired a local string quartet (how she was able to get them on Christmas Eve I'll never know but God bless her she did). They were instructed to begin playing when the sun went down. Peeking out the window I could see the fires going, the white lights twinkling everywhere. The girls had strung one million white lights over where we would be married. Every path was lit up and there were so many Christmas trees and poinsettias you couldn't count them all, it was glorious. So much better than I could ever have imagined.

A day I'll never forget. A memory to last a lifetime.

Sophie was gorgeous in her beautiful red dress. Her and Francesca's girls were dressed in red satin ankle-length dresses with white lace peeking from the bottom. I noticed Sophie had the same pearl and rough-cut ruby pendant around her neck as the rings we were given. And then I saw that Francesca's girls had them as well. My heart swelled and I almost let a tear go... but I knew Terra and Jenna would kill me if I cried and ruined my makeup. The knowledge that Sophie and Francesca's daughters were carrying on some of our traditions... along with creating their own with each other was perfect.

The best wedding present a mother could ask for.

I peeked around the large tree and saw the ladies seated in the front row of the arbor. I also saw that Laird was there waiting. My handsome husband-to-be was fidgeting with his bow tie.

I smiled.

This is the best day of my life and I almost didn't want it to come to an end. Once I walk down that aisle it would be the beginning of the end of the day. But I consoled myself that it was the beginning of the rest of my life with the man that meant everything to me.

Everything.

I stole another moment to look around at the long bridal table and how beautifully it was decorated. The round guest tables were filled with people. The beautiful miniature three-tiered wedding cakes sat in the center with white miniature lights around the base and red roses cascading down one side. Large red candelabras rose up from either side of the cake. The white boa wreaths on the backs of the chairs with the red velvet ribbon were exquisite. Everything sparkled and glowed and was magical. Exactly how a Christmas wedding should be. I glanced over at the fire pit area where Francesca had placed faux fur throws and pillows for the guests to recline after dinner.

The horse-drawn carriage had delivered the last of the wedding guests and was being tended to. They would stay for photographs after the ceremony and return the guests to their cars afterward.

I took in the whiskey bar, the vodka bar with the giant ice sculpture, the champagne fountain, and the chocolate fountain, absolutely everything was perfect. My song began and I felt good butterflies for the first time in a long while. I knew it was my time to get a move on but I was savoring every second. I would take this moment to my grave. This day would be the day I remembered on my last day when my life flashed before my eyes, this would be the top. I couldn't imagine anything better.

Crystals hung from twisted pearl garlands that were intertwined with white fairy lights and strung elegantly overhead. I moved to the door and then outside.

The music played on and as I walked closer to the aisle where everybody would be able to see me. I placed my beautiful red rose bouquet in front of my dress and started the last walk as a single woman, to the man of my dreams. When my guests saw me they rose and for a moment I caught Francesca's eye and thought I saw tears. I wanted to rush up to her and ask her if she thought Frank would have liked this. But I already knew the answer.

So I didn't.

Instead, I looked at my future husband and saw that his eyes were trained on me. A flush washed over my body. This was my man, this was going to be my husband and the look he was giving me was one of love... with something else mixed in that I couldn't quite place.

That is until he decided I was taking too long making my way down the aisle.

He growled, "Angel," Before he stormed down the aisle until he stood in front of me. Ah, the look was impatience.

Another look washed over his face and his eyes watered.

"You are the most beautiful woman I have ever seen in my entire life and if you don't get your ass down this aisle and marry me right now my head's gonna explode."

I laughed out loud because that was the last thing I expected him to say. But I should've known, this was my guy after all. He was not big on pomp and circumstance.

He was a "just the facts ma'am" kind of guy. And I loved that about him. There was only room for one diva and that was me. It was good that we both knew that going in.

I smiled up at him and laid my hand on his chest. "Why don't you walk me down the aisle and let's have our wedding be the way we will live our married life, side-by-side, my hand in yours forever."

"That's the best thing I've heard all day." He moved to my side. I wove my hand through his bent arm and together we walked down the aisle to where our daughter Sophie, and Laird were waiting for us.

The ceremony was short and sweet; we didn't have grandiose vows to exchange. Not in front of everybody anyway, our vows would be exchanged in private in the hotel honeymoon suite at the local Vines and Roses Inn.

The reception was incredible. I think it went on until four am even though it was Christmas Eve. There was so much food and festivities, and the music and magic of the evening no one wanted to leave.

I stole a moment away from Roman, he'd been keeping a close eye on me. I don't think he was totally convinced that Lydia was on our side. To be honest I wasn't a hundred percent convinced she was either, but now that we were married there was nothing she could do. We couldn't be her focus anymore there would be no reason.

I found Francesca curled around Laird in front of a fire pit with a blanket over them making out like a couple of teenagers. At first, I felt awkward interrupting them. But then I thought no, this was my wedding if I'm ever gonna be rude and a buttinsky ... this was the place I could do it.

I was the only one wearing white so it was pretty hard to miss me but these two somehow managed. They were so engrossed with each other that they had no idea I'd even approached. It was starting to get a little awkward, so I cleared my throat. Then, when they showed no signs of slowing down, I cleared my throat again.

And when that still didn't work, I said, "Hey! You two need to get a room."

Francesca jumped like a teenager who'd been caught making out with her boyfriend at the front door. Laird, well there's just no other way to say it. He had the biggest shit-eating grin on his face I'd ever seen in my entire life.

And I've seen a lot of shit-eating grins.

"Hey sis, I'm just checking to make sure you're okay?" I asked softly then glanced at Laird.

Laird gave me another big grin.

"Aye lass, she is more than fine. But I'll let her tell ye all about it. For now, I'm off to grab champagne and give you two a couple of minutes alone." He leaned over and kissed her head, then strode away. There was no other way to describe his walk. Clad in his kilt, big heavy boots and tuxedo jacket he made quite a picture with his long aggressive strides.

I began to turn to her and took a double take. I could've sworn I saw a skip in his step. We quietly watched Francesca's fine man, while holding our conversation, because that's just what you had to do. He was that fine.

Of course, not as fine as Roman in my opinion, but I could sure see where Francesca might think he looked just as good... if not better.

"Well?" I asked.

Her smile was almost shy.

"I was going to wait to tell you tomorrow." She looked past me, "all of you. I don't want to do anything to take away from your day, Sydney." She took my hands into hers. "Look around. This is the most magical day I've ever seen here. I'm just so thankful that you let me host your wedding. You've given us the gift of creating happy memories...to help dim some of the bad that we've lived through the last few years." I watched a tear track down her face and my breath caught. "The girls and I need happiness." She was whispering as if the words were too painful to be said aloud. "The girls and I, we need happiness. It has to be okay for us to move on. Even if it means moving on without him... without Frank."

"Oh honey," I gripped her hands. "Nobody wants you to suffer. You and the girls hurting and living miserable lives isn't going to bring Frank back. That man loved you with everything in him. The last thing he would want would be for you to torture yourself."

She gave me a watery smile. "I do actually have something I'm dying to tell you. I was going to wait, but I think I need to do it today. I hope you don't mind."

"Well, now you have to tell me." I smiled. She looked past me again and then looked down shyly.

What was up with all this shyness?

Francesca held up her left hand. On her ring finger sat an exquisite blue aquamarine surrounded by diamonds, and set in white gold. It had an unusual shape, was multifaceted, and with the white lights around us and the glow of the fire, it was casting flares against her face.

My eyes met hers and we shared a brief second before Becca yelled, "Woo hoo we're going to have another wedding!" We shared a smile before I was shouldered aside as Becca and Jenna pushed past me to "oh and ah" over Francesca's ring.

As the other girls gathered around to share in the wonderful news Laird returned and the men gravitated toward us as well. I felt my husband's strong arms engulf me. I breathed in his spice along with the scent of whiskey. I settled in and rested my body against his.

"You having fun, baby?" Roman growled in my ear.

"I think this might be the happiest night of my life." I turned in his arms and laid my head against his chest. "Merry Christmas, husband."

"Merry Christmas, Angel."

Wrapped up in my husband's arms, surrounded by my friend's happiness I realized that I had the best Christmas present ever. One I'd never have been brave enough to ask for... but one I am so thankful to receive.

32

And Laughter

"This is marvelous! I've not seen anythin' like it befor'!" The large red-faced man bellowed. We were strolling with Laird's newly arrived parents through the flocked Christmas tree forest Francesca had created.

"It's all very impressive. Festive." Laird's father was a robust man with a loud voice and a deep laugh. His mother, an American transplant, was so small next to her husband that they almost didn't fit. Until you saw him look at her. Then you knew without a shadow of a doubt that they fit.

We'd already had a puff from the cigar bar, tasted the whiskey, drank a shot of Russian vodka from the ice sculpture, and were currently traipsing through the Christmas tree forest on our way to the chocolate fountain.

Francesca and Laird were arm-in-arm taking up the lead. Next up, Roman and I, Sophie, Faith, and Fallon were trailing behind, and after them were Laird's parents; who refused to tell us their first names. They insisted we refer to them as Nanna and Grandpa Hamilton. Lastly, Jenna and Marcus took up the rear.

Laird's parents were so overjoyed that their son had finally chosen a wife that they had come straight away.

Nanna Hamilton stroked Faith's head lovingly.

"After scaring us half to death that he'd never give us any grand-children, the least he could do was reward his parents with you two lovelies. I am going to spoil you rotten and I don't care one bit how that sounds!" Faith liked the way that sounded and smiled big at her new Nanna.

Apparently, as soon as Laird had shared his plans to propose his parents began making arrangements to come for Christmas. As they said there was no way they were missing out on their new family; they had grandchildren to spoil and no time to spare.

I honestly thought having my wedding on Christmas Eve meant that it would be a quick ceremony, with a quick dinner and people would be eager to disperse to their own homes to prepare for Christmas morning. But that's not what happened. I think maybe three guests left and everybody else stayed. The champagne flowed, the vodka flowed, and the whiskey was poured. The cigar bar was a big hit but surprisingly mostly with the female guests.

"I'm ready to get our honeymoon started." Roman wrapped his arm around my shoulders and curled me into him.

I felt warm, secure, and safe. One of the best feelings of my life. "Let me say goodbye to my girls and then we can leave. You were in charge of the honeymoon. What did you have planned?"

As we rounded the corner through the Christmas tree forest and it opened up to a sea of white and cream poinsettias, something was going on near the champagne fountain.

Terra threw her champagne glass on the ground in a very unlike Terra move. I glanced at the man standing next to her, his face was red, and he was stiff and stoic. Terra swung around and I got the first look at her face. It was filled with utter grief. I let go of Roman and went to where she was standing. Jenna and Francesca hot on my heels. The three of us arrived where Terra was running away from Sebastian.

"Babe," I was out of breath. "Stop, I can't keep up with you in this dress."

Terra slowed her walk but didn't stop fully. She looked over at me and I could see the pain written across her face.

"What's happening?" I closed in and put my arm around her waist and pulled her to me. Jenna and Francesca closed in on the other side of her and we directed her away from the wedding and towards Francesca's house.

"Wait, I don't want all of us to leave Sydney's wedding." She stopped. "I just need a few minutes to gather my wits about me. I'm not really ready to talk about what's upsetting me." She turned her back to us. "Just give me a minute."

"Nope!" Jenna obviously had enough of waiting. "Not here. Not now. It's Sydney's wedding." She pointed at me and then at Francesca. "This one got a proposal. That's enough."

I knew Jenna was just trying to be thoughtful. But there was very little that could happen that would screw up how amazing this day was even the fact that I hadn't had sleep in almost two days.

I took Terra's hands in mine. "We're here to share the good and the bad. So lay it on me sister, what's going on?"

Terra turned her back on us briefly, when she turned back her face was stoic.

"You guys are going to be a little surprised to hear this. I've had a thing for Sebastian since I first laid eyes on him. I thought he felt the same."

Against my will, laughter broke free.

"Girl, we've all known. We left it alone because we figured you'd tell us when you were ready. Plus, we've had a lot going on, too. But mostly sis, we were waiting for you to be ready to tell us. From my recollection, you've not been interested in dating much at all. Now, I know I'd been gone for six years but even then you never talked about dating and when I asked if you were dating the answer was always no."

Terra gave me a soft look. "It's true. I haven't been interested in dating. I just needed a break from men when I moved here. Then it became a habit to avoid them. And honestly, nobody struck my fancy." Her eyes flipped to where Sebastian was standing next to Lydia. My eyes followed her gaze And I understood where the issue lay.

"Lydia's not a problem." I loved the idea of Terra and Sebastian together. I'd been waiting for them to get their act together and make a move, or at least share with the rest of us what they were doing if anything.

"I wish that were true. I heard her convincing Sebastian to marry her. He didn't seem resistant to the idea until he noticed me listening."

I could see how this would be a problem. It would seem perfectly normal for Lydia, from Lydia's perspective, to marry somebody like Sebastian whom she could trust. The girls didn't know the issues that she was facing back home, or that I had volunteered to help her. But we would need to lay down some ground rules with Lydia before we got started. And one of them would be hands-off of Sebastian.

"I'll talk to Lydia. This may be a little bit my fault, I suggested she marry somebody else and not go back home until she had. I think her life is in danger... or will be."

"This is why I don't date. Men are untrustworthy." Terra looked at me with big eyes as she realized what she'd said - to my face - on my wedding day.

"It's okay honey," I said. " I know what's happened and I know where you come from. I know how far you've come along. Nobody's trying to get you to do anything that you don't want to do. And your experience is not going to be my experience. Roman is a one-of-a-kind type of guy and if I wasn't marrying him I probably wouldn't be getting married at all. So don't worry about watching your words with me now."

"Thank you for that. But I'm afraid this just reaffirms my stance on staying away from men. All they do is hurt you, steal from you, and ruin everything good that you have in your life."

Thankfully Roman chose that moment to interrupt.

"Are you about ready?" He snuggled my neck.

"I haven't had any of the chocolate fountain yet. That makes me sad." I snuggled back.

"The chocolate fountain it is."

33

Until Death Do Us Part

Guess where Roman took us on our honeymoon?

Vegas.

Yes, that's what I said. The man booked us the honeymoon suite at the Bellagio in Las Vegas.

Now, Vegas with my girls would've been amazing...

Vegas on my honeymoon?

Not so much. The perfect honeymoon for me would be a fancy house on a tropical island isolated away from everybody else. Make out under a waterfall. Swim naked in a lagoon. Enjoy the beach and a plethora of umbrella drinks.

Not one of the busiest cities in the world, crammed full of people.

But then... he opened the door to this huge gorgeous room packed full of red, yellow, pink, and white roses. Flowers were everywhere and they were out of this world. No one had ever done anything like that for me before.

I walked in speechless and touched every bouquet.

"Thank you." I gave him a watery smile. He kicked the staff out of the room and carried me to the bed where he proceeded to ravage me. It wasn't our first tryst as a married couple, but it was the sweetest. We took some time and enjoyed each other... until the room phone rang alerting us that the masseuses were on their way and we had to hurry through our showers. I would have preferred to take my time. But the massages were a great way to kick off our honeymoon.

I was almost finished getting ready for dinner. It was our second night at the hotel. The reservations were for seven.

This was our first time leaving the suite since we'd arrived. And even though this wasn't my first choice for a destination, being with him was all that mattered. That, and I would be making all of the future vacation choices.

Thankfully he'd arranged a dinner for us out of our room. And it was some swanky affair because he'd gifted me a new dress for the occasion and it was close-your-mouth gorgeous. The skirt fell to the floor in a sleek sheath and a modest back slit. It clung where you wanted but also offered a little movement so it felt comfortable. The spaghetti straps and deep back made me think of my girl Jenna.

She'd love it.

I stepped back and snapped a photo of my reflection, then quickly texted her with a bunch of silly emojis. She immediately texted back *"Love the Bordeaux color!"* I texted back a heart, a kissy face, and another heart.

The suite was stunning. We had incredible views of Las Vegas, with a private pool on our private balcony. He'd ordered endless amounts of champagne and an in-room couples massage an hour after we'd arrived. Nothing like starting the honeymoon outright.

Entering the living area, I found Roman standing in front of the floor-length window gazing out over the city.

Chills washed over me and my breath caught. This was real. I had been in a sleep-deprived, stressed-induced fog for the entire wedding. But now the reality of it all was hitting me.

This was real.

He was mine.

We were really and truly a couple. We were married, and the wedding was incredible. My man was romantic and sexy, and the best part was... he was all mine. I didn't have to share him with anyone.

I slid my arms around Roman's stomach and laid my head on his back.

"This is lovely." I closed my eyes and soaked in his masculinity.

"But you'd have preferred an isolated beach somewhere tropical?" A small smile played over my face. He turned to face me and engulfed me in his arms. I rested my cheek against his chest.

"Anywhere we are together is the right place for me." I pulled back to look up at his handsome face. "Do you have enough money to buy an island?"

Instead of answering he changed the subject. I squinted at him to indicate this topic wasn't done but I'd let it go for now.

"I can't quit thinking about Lydia taking you... and me not being there..." He rested his chin on my head. "When we get back, I'm having a serious talk with Aleks about those daughters of his."

Roman was still upset about having to spend the night before his wedding up a tree. I smiled but hid it from him. His cousins had avoided Roman throughout the wedding and reception. It was good to know that they had some survival instincts, at the rate they were going they were going to need them.

"Let's get food for us. I'm starving."

We headed to the private dining room set aside for special guests. The room was just off of the wine cellar that most guests never got to see. I noticed the large double doors with gold hardware right away. I'd never been in this room myself but had clients who had been so fortunate to have dined there. It was said to be a once-in-a-lifetime experience.

The maître d' threw the doors open and the greeting inside had me first yell... then slap Roman's chest! I laughed but that quickly dissolved into tears.

They were there. All of them.

Becca, Terra, Jenna and Marcus, Sloane, Stella, Juliette, Isabella and Cabe, Sophie, Susan, Francesca and Laird, Faith and Fallon, Laird's parents... everyone I loved was right here.

My family.

"I thought this might help make up for the bullshit you had to put up with." Roman hadn't removed his hands from me since we'd said our "I do's"

"This is perfect. But baby, this isn't the honeymoon you wanted. I know you love them... but I also know you wanted us alone."

"This isn't our honeymoon."

"It's not?"

"No. Our honeymoon starts two days from today when we fly out to St. Barts so you can feel the sun on your ass like you really wanted."

"St Barts, you say?"

He nodded, watching me closely.

"I think they have topless beaches." I smiled as seductively as I could muster.

Roman growled and pulled me closer. "I'll get us a private beach if you want to go topless. Hell, you can go naked. But only for me, wife."

I liked the way that word sounded coming from him.

"Say it again," I whispered.

"Wife."

"You get me a private beach and I'll spend all day on it as naked as the day I was born." I was sort of joking and sort of telling the truth. I wanted to be free enough to go topless but my American upbringing might make me feel conflicted.

The look on his face made me flush and rethink the entire conversation.

"Challenge accepted."

Fan Fiction

*Below is a wonderful short story by Bernadine Chapman-Cruz.
This fun read has nothing to do with the couple's storyline in the
series... but I absolutely LOVE that she wrote about my favorite
couple and wanted you all to get a giggle too!*
Enjoy!
xoxo Terry

Sydney had been procrastinating over Harmony Grove's Law Enforcement annual recognition dinner for the past month. She didn't want to go, yet she knew she had to make an appearance to support her handsome husband Roman. Once again, he was one of the honored guests for his ongoing contributions to the community.

Roman didn't like being in the spotlight either, however, felt it his duty to at least make an appearance. A former California Highway Patrolman, whose background also included bodyguarding and sniffing out Russian Mob activity, he now owned a high-tech security business. His new endeavor never failed to put him in the right place at the right time when police radios screeched in on a hot pursuit. More often than not, Roman beat the cops to the scene. He had become a legend when it came to catching the bad guys. If it wasn't her husband's reputation as a lone ranger when it came to solving a crime that put his life on the line, he also had an acute intuition that put him smack dab in the middle of danger. But she couldn't blame him for his contributions to law and order. Her career as an attorney also brought unwanted recognition. She too, unwittingly found herself embroiled in dangerous, even life escapades.

"Let's go, Babe," Roman called from the foyer. "We're going to be late."

Sydney took a final look in the full-length mirror, flipped her hair to the side, and reluctantly headed downstairs.

"You look lovely. I wish we didn't have to go tonight. I'd be just as happy to capture you in a cops and robbers scenario right here at home and see where it takes us." A devilish grin spread across Roman's face as he bent down to kiss his wife. Just his closeness brought that tingling sensation Sydney knew so well. This man, she thought. I can never get enough of him.

"Me too," Sydney whispered into his ear, as he gently gave her a squeeze before pushing her out the door.

When they arrived at the venue, all heads turned. They definitely were a striking couple, complimenting each other in every way, both in public and private. The women swooned at Roman's command of the room. Men envied him for his choice of partner as Sydney was a strikingly beautiful woman. If there was a marriage made in heaven, they were the couple.

Stopping at the bar, they ordered drinks and made the rounds greeting friends and associates, before finding their designated table. Sydney looked up at Roman as he pulled out her chair. The magnetism was as strong as ever. How did I get so lucky, she thought as she slid into her seat. Roman pulled out the adjacent chair and sat down, giving her a peck on the cheek. Her perfume was one of his favorites.

Sydney was completely drawn in. She reached out and grabbed Roman's thigh under the table. Nobody will see, she assured herself. The fiery touch of his tight-fitting trousers left nothing to the imagination. She could feel his muscles ripple beneath the fabric. It was like magic. She was his and he was hers, body and soul. Sydney closed her eyes, drinking in the sensation.

Instantaneously, Sydney was thrown back to the night they met. Her chest rose as she took a deep breath. She could feel her heart pounding. A warm sensation spread from her chest to her neck filtering up to her cheeks. She felt hot. She was blushing. Her memories engulfed her.

The hum of the room, seemed far away, as she was brought full circle back to the searing emotions of their first encounter on the ground at the side of the interstate. Fear, helplessness, and an unabashed need to save his life. Sydney remembered feeling Roman's warm red blood pulsing through his body. Her heart was racing like wildfire ready to jump out of her chest.

That night, however, the emotions were solely hers, not Roman's, as he lay unconscious. He was bleeding profusely from a gunshot wound. Little did Sydney realize that she was about to save the life of her soulmate. Seared in her mind, was the man's masculine physique, warm body, and blood gushing everywhere. How would she stop the bleeding?

With nothing on the roadside, the only thing she had were her hands. In shock, she had enough sense to realize that she had to find the wound. Sydney pressed on the unconscious man's bloody clothing covering a well-defined taught body feeling every inch. She was frightened but had to save his life. Exploring his close-to-lifeless form, she found the wound in his groin area. With trembling but determined fingers, Sydney unbuckled his belt, undid his zipper, pulled the fabric of his uniform pants apart at the waist, and shoved her fingers into the wound. But to penetrate the wound, she had to push his enormous manly parts aside. Even in her state of panic, she realized this guy was something special. He was hung.

Around her, Sydney heard muffled table talk, but still, in a world of her own, she was caught in the memories of the past moving her further away from the present. In her state of confusion the only thing she knew she had to do, was to save this man's life. Fuzzy, Sydney thought she heard Roman's name. The emcee called for Roman to approach the head table to receive his award.

Roman knew his time had come and attempted to push back in his chair but Sydney couldn't remove her hands from his genitalia. He would surely bleed out. She felt him trying to pull away from her to stand up. But in her deep, all-encompassing memory, she knew she couldn't let go, just as she didn't let go the night she heard the sirens of the ambulance racing to the scene of the accident the night they met.

Roman was taken aback, as he tried to loosen himself from his wife's vice-like grip on his crotch. Sydney wouldn't – she couldn't let go. She hung on for dear life – his life. She had to keep the pressure on the pulsating blood spurting from his groin. Embarrassed, Roman tried to push her hands away, but to no avail. He was locked in her grip, bent over the table unable to stand. Embarrassed, he realized standing wasn't the only problem. Under Sydney's pleasurable pressure on his manhood, he was getting an erection. With a violent jerk backward, he shot up pulling Sydney with him, still squeezing his crotch. There they stood in the most embarrassing moment in their lives. It was definitely a night to remember.

About the Author

T Wells Brown grew up in the deep south, chasing frogs (kissing one or two), catching crawdads from the local creek (much to her mother's dismay), and traipsing through poison ivy (half her childhood was spent covered in calamine lotion).

She now lives in the lush California Zinfandel wine country with the Love of Her Life and their two rescued pups. Pups she often writes into her books. T Wells Brown is the author of the romantic suspense series; Women of Wine Country, the contemporary fantasy series; Earth Magic, and the international collaboration; Sisters of Sin. She is also the feature writer for Best Version Media; a community magazine.

Besides reading, writing, and wine guzzling, she devotes her time to her small community, her wine tribe sisterhood, feeding, and re-homing the plethora of homeless pets in the community, and promoting women's issues. Halloween, she dances as one of the Witches of Wine Country with her tribe. Two months later she trades the pointy black hat in for a red dress, and she can often be found impersonating Mrs. Claus.

Would you like to contact Ms. Wells-Brown? You can email her at twellsbrown@gmail.com

You can connect with me on:

🌐 https://twellsbrown.com

🐦 https://twitter.com/twellsbrown

📘 https://www.facebook.com/authorwellsbrown

🔗 https://www.facebook.com/groups/845893239187012

Subscribe to my newsletter:

✉ https://twellsbrown.com/terrys-tribe

Also by T Wells Brown

Thank you for reading **Lawyer & Lace**. If you enjoyed it would you please leave a review for the book on your favorite book site? Forever grateful, it helps us so much.

If you haven't yet read Sydney & Roman's story, you can find it below. **Her Escape** and **Catalina** are free stories I hope you'll enjoy. You can use the QR code or the link. Last on the list is **Vanity**, the first book in a six-book **femme fatale** series.

If for any reason the links don't work, please visit my website @ twellsbrown.com where you'll find these books, plus many more.

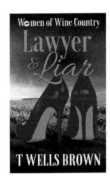

Lawyer & Lace

https://twellsbrown.com/earth-magic

Officer down!

Those two words loop over and over in my head, every-single-day since I found a sexy-as-heck man bleeding out on the side of the highway.

Not just any man.

Oh no, of course not. It had to be a Big Strong Sexy Alpha Man; my kryptonite. It gets worse when he figures out how attracted I am to him and uses it to his advantage.

Never trust a man who doesn't play fair.

Saving his life changed everything in mine. And not for the good.

Now, I'm on the run. I never dreamed, in all my boring days, I'd find myself running from the Russian Mafia! How the heck did I end up here?

All I can say is that Big Strong Sexy Alpha Man better figure it out, and fast! Because these men mean business!

Bad business.

Her Escape

https://bookhip.com/SSSWQHV

Sometimes a gal just needs a couple of days to herself.

Was that too much to ask? No?

I didn't think so either. So, I did the unthinkable, took those days, and headed up to my favorite hideaway in the mountains.

Blue skies and sparkling waterfalls. Just what the doctor ordered. Everything was going fine until he appeared in my rear view mirror.

A Dark Knight riding a black beast and hot on my tail. But was he a true Dark Knight? With my luck? Probably not.

Unfortunately for me, people are rarely what they seem. He just may be the very thing I needed to escape from. Also, he was one of the largest men I'd ever seen and was riding the biggest motorcycle on the road.

Have Mercy.

CATALINA

I wasn't born an elite assassin removing the worst types of men from the world.

I wasn't born an elite assassin removing the worst types of men from the world.

I became this version of myself by learning the hard way how little justice there is in the world for those who can't fight for themselves.

No one can ever say I sat back on my haunches when those who needed me most were hurt or worse. Enter Mother and the Sisters of Sin who not only took me in but taught me how to be as badass as I could be.

VANITY

https://twellsbrown.com/earth-magic

Deadly. Beautiful. Rich. Sinful.

Assassins are the stuff of children's games, until you grow up and realize the fairy tales are all true.

Monsters do exist.

They come in the form of bad men doing very bad things, who go unchecked for their crimes against the innocent.

Until now.

My name is Catalina Willow, aka Vanity.

Two items you should know about me; I'm an elite assassin, and I like nice things.

Luckily, killing bad people pays very well. Life was going perfectly. I kept my head down, took my assignments, and I never ever looked back.

That is, until I'm asked to remove an influential head of state. Apparently, my assignment's security team didn't appreciate how good I was at my job and decided to hunt me down.

Commander Juan Carlos Cortez, was the baddest of the bad, and he was hot on my stiletto-studded trail.

But I didn't become one of the best assassins in my sisterhood by being soppy… or weak.

I decided it was time for a change and believed I'd outwitted him… until he arrived on the small tropical island where I happened to be executing my newest assignment.

I don't believe in coincidences, so I took my wins, and hightailed it off the island.

Now, I'm on the run of my life … and enjoying every moment of it.

Men. Sex. Sin.

We ruin the rules and revel in it.

We are the Sisters of Sin.

Join me, as I dive into an elite assassin organization. One dedicated to bringing justice to the world, one kill at a time.

Made in United States
Orlando, FL
06 December 2022